A Bachelor's Dream

Margaret Wolfe Hungerford

A BACHELOR'S DREAM

CHAPTER I.

"Now what can be done?" said the Doctor. "That's the question. What on earth can I do about it?"

He put this question emphatically, with an energetic blow of his gloved hand upon his knee, and seemed very desirous of receiving an answer, although he was jogging along alone in his comfortable brougham. But the Doctor was perplexed, and wanted some one to help him out of his difficulty. He was a bachelor, and knew therefore that it was of no use letting Patrick drive him home in search of a confidant, for at home the ruling genius of his household was his housekeeper, Mrs. Jessop. She was a most excellent creature, an invaluable manager of the house, the tradespeople, and the maid-servants, and a splendid cook; the Doctor appreciated her highly, but he was not disposed to ask her advice or to invite her consolation.

He beat his knee a little harder, frowned more severely; finally let down the window, put out his head, and called smartly:

"Patrick!"

"Sir." Patrick pulled up the slim, clean-limbed brown horse as quickly as he could in the midst of the hurrying vehicles and hucksters' stalls which are usually to be found in the Essex Road at about seven o'clock on Saturday evening, and looked questioningly down at his master.

"Don't go home. Drive me to Petersham Villa," said Dr. Brudenell.

Patrick obeyed rather sulkily. He did not know what his master could possibly want at Petersham Villa—where he had already been once that day—and he did know that he himself was exceedingly hungry, and desirous of getting home. He gave the brown horse an undeserved cut over the ears with his whip; and when he pulled up he did so with a jerk which he might easily have avoided.

"I sha'n't be many minutes," said the Doctor, alighting in front of a comfortable-looking well-kept house, with red gleams of firelight shining from its parlor windows. "Walk the horse up and down to keep the cold off, but don't go far."

"It's cowld enough we'll both be, I'm thinkin'," muttered Patrick, gathering up the reins with a shiver; for it was really a very cold evening indeed, damp and gray, with a biting east wind.

If the Doctor heard this complaint, he did not heed it, his policy being, when his henchman was attacked with a fit of grumbling, to let him recover his good-temper at his leisure. He had hurried up the snow-white flight of steps, given a vigorous knock at the door, and, being admitted by a neat maid-servant, was asking if Mrs. Leslie were at home. Hearing that she was, he crossed the hall with an air of being perfectly at home, and, after tapping at the door, entered the parlor, causing a lady who was making tea to utter an exclamation of surprise, and a young lady who was making toast before the glowing fire to drop a deliciously-browned slice of bread into the cinders.

"Why, Doctor"—the tea-maker extended a plump hand good-naturedly—"you again? You are just in time for a cup of tea. I believe you came on purpose."

"Hardly that; but I shall be glad of one, if I may have it, Mrs. Leslie," the Doctor returned, emulating her light tone as well as he could; and, after shaking hands with the younger lady, who got up from her knees to greet him, he took a seat near the round table, not in the well-worn, cozy arm-chair in the snuggest corner of the snug room, which, with its gorgeous dressing-gown thrown across it and slippers warming before the fire, wad evidently sacred to somebody else.

"Of course—although I fancy you rather despise it as a rule. Not a bit like my Tom!"

"Ah, you see I'm not like Tom in having some one to make it for me!"

"Well, that's your fault, I suppose," said the lively woman, vivaciously, as she deftly handled the shining copper kettle. "I told Kate it was your knock; but she wouldn't believe that you could honor us with two visits in one day."

"I thought Doctor Brudenell's time was too valuable," observed Kate, quietly, as she resumed her toasting.

She was not nearly so pretty as her sister, although Mrs. Leslie was the elder of the two by twelve years. Maria Leslie had taken life so easily, and turned such a bright face to all its ups and downs, that time had rewarded her at forty by making her look six or seven years younger. A downright pretty woman she was, bright-eyed, bright-cheeked, bright-haired, and so plump and merry that it was a pleasure to look at her. Kate Merritt was smaller, darker, more grave, and less attractive altogether. Doctor Brudenell liked them both, but he preferred the elder, as most people did. He enjoyed a visit to Petersham Villa—it was almost the only house with whose inhabitants he was upon really easy and familiar terms, for he was by nature a shy and retiring man. He had got into the habit of confiding in cheerful Mrs. Leslie, but he seldom talked to Kate, who was too diffident to make him forget that he also was inclined to be shy. Indeed he thought so little about her that he had not even a suspicion that in her quiet, cool, self-controlled, persistent way, she had made up her mind to marry him. Mrs. Leslie did know it, and often rated her sister soundly on the subject, with even a touch of contempt sometimes.

"You are most absurd to keep that silly notion fixed in your head!" she would declare, impatiently. "He doesn't care a straw for you, child! Haven't you wit enough to see that? If he only knew what a goose you were he'd pay you the compliment of thinking you crazy, I tell you. He's a good fellow—the best fellow in the world after my Tom—but there's something odd about him in that way. Can't you see that he hardly knows one woman from another, you silly child? I don't, for my part, believe that the man has ever been in love in his life at all."

Mrs. Leslie was penetrative, but in this matter she was wrong; for, if George Brudenell had been asked, he would probably have confessed that he had been in love twice. True, his first passion had been conceived at the age of eighteen, its object being the bosom-friend of his only sister, a young lady who owned to six-and-twenty, and who had laughed at him mercilessly when the most startling of valentines had made her aware of the state of things. Then, years after, when he was nearly thirty, he had become very fond of the daughter of his partner, a pretty, gentle, winning creature some half a dozen years younger than himself, who had girlishly adored him. He had been so fond of her and so used to her, he had grieved so sincerely when, a month before what was to have been their wedding-day, she died, that he did not realize in the least that he had reached his present age of forty-three without having been really in love at all.

He was not unhappy. A studious man, cold, taciturn, and self-contained as a rule, caring little for general society and devoted to his profession, the want in his life, the blank in his wifeless and childless home, was not to him what it would have been to a more impulsive, less self-reliant nature. If sometimes he instituted an involuntary comparison between his contracted hoped and interests as contrasted with those of other men, books, his work, his studies, soon consoled him. He hardly knew there was a yearning in his breast—a vague, intangible felling, waiting for a mistress-hand to stir it into activity—the hand of a woman whom he had never seen.

"And what brings you here a second time, Doctor?" asked Mrs. Leslie, brightly, as she poured out a cup of tea and handed it to him. "Are you going to give us some advice gratis?"

"Hardly, Mrs. Leslie; in fact, I want yours."

"Mine?" exclaimed the lady, vivaciously. "It is yours, of course—but upon what subject?"

"This. You recollect that I told you my sister was coming home from India with her children?"

"To be sure—I remember. Well?"

"Well, I have a letter from her announcing that, as she has been out of health for the last month or two, her husband does not wish her to travel yet. But her children are coming to England—they are on their way, in fact, and coming to me."

Doctor Brudenell, in making this statement, did not feel comical, but he looked so, in spite of his grave, refined, scholarly face, and Mrs. Leslie greeted his words with a burst of hearty laughter.

"My dear Doctor, don't look so tragic! The poor little creatures won't eat you. So they are coming to you? Well, what is your difficulty?"

"Merely, what am I to do with them?"

"Why, take care of them, of course!"

The Doctor stirred his tea with an air of helpless bewilderment. He felt that this was all very well as far as it went, and strictly what he meant to do, of course; but it did not go far enough—it was no solution of his difficulty. He felt a distinct sense of injury, too. His sister had got married, which was all very well. She had had eight children, only three of whom were now alive; and it occurred to him that, having the children, it was clearly Laura's duty to look after them. There was en element of coolness in her sending them to him which he found rather disconcerting. It opened a prospect of unending domestic tribulation. Laura herself had been an altogether irrepressible child, loud in voice, restless of movement, tireless of tongue, insatiable in curiosity, unceasing in mischief. What would his quiet house be with three editions of Laura running rampant about it? They would invade his study, disarrange his books, frolic in the drawing-room, make quiet and peace things of the past. What could he do with them? What would Mrs. Jessop say? The Doctor shuddered at the thought; the prospect appalled him.

"You had better get a governess for them," suggested Mrs. Leslie, briskly.

"A governess!" This was a ray of light, but he was not sure that he did not prefer darkness. "Oh—a governess?" he repeated, interrogatively.

"Of course! They will be tiresome, you may be sure—all children are, and Anglo-Indian ones particularly—at least so I should fancy—and you certainly will not want them disturbing you, while it will never do to have them running riot over the house.

Get a good, sensible, responsible person, not too young, and you will find that you need hardly be troubled at all."

The Doctor felt that this counsel was good. It was plain, practical, feasible. But there remained a difficulty. How was he to become possessed of the sensible, responsible person who was not too young?

"Advertise," suggested his adviser, tersely.

Of course! How very foolish of him not to have thought of it! The plainest possible way out of the dilemma.

"Thank you, Mrs. Leslie," said the Doctor, rising and taking up his hat. "Thank you. I've no doubt that you're perfectly right. I will advertise."

He shook hands with the ladies—gratefully with the one, indifferently with the other—and bowed himself out, hurrying to the waiting Patrick, who had fulfilled his own prophecy in so far that he was by this time "cowld" in every limb, although his temper was exceedingly warm.

From the window Kate Merritt watched the brougham roll away and then turned to her sister angrily, tears in her eyes, a hot flush upon her face. Although she was by nature really obstinate, resolute, and persistent, she often exhibited upon the surface a childish pettishness with which her real self was almost absurdly at variance. She spoke now as a spoilt child might have done.

"How dreadfully disagreeable you are, Maria! It's too bad, I declare! I believe you do it on purpose—there!"

"Do what on purpose? What in the world do you mean?" cried Mrs. Leslie, pausing, sugar-tongs in hand.

"You know what I mean!" exclaimed Kate, scarcely able to suppress a sob.

"I declare I do not. This is some fad about Doctor Brudenell, I suppose," said the elder sister, resignedly. "Do me the favor to be intelligible, at least, Kate. What is it that you mean?"

"Why did you advise him to advertise?" demanded Miss Merritt.

"Because it was the most sensible advice I could give him. Is that the grievance? What objection have you to his advertising?"

"That I know very well what it will come to. He'll take your advice, and advertise, and get some woman into his house who will pet the children and coax and wheedle him until she gets completely round him, and then we know what will happen," cried Kate, with her handkerchief pressed to her eyes.

Mrs. Leslie looked at her, and had some difficulty in restraining a laugh.

"Nonsense, child! Doctor Brudenell will no more fall in love with his governess than he will with anybody else. For goodness' sake do try to be more sensible. A nice opinion of you he would have if he could only hear and see you now, I must say! I should be ashamed, if I were you, to spend my time fretting and crying after a man who didn't care a pin about me, like a love-sick school-girl. Dry your eyes and come to the table. Whoever the poor man gets for a governess, I hope she may have more common sense than you, I am sure. And the sooner he advertises for her the better, if that unruly brood is to be here so soon."

"He would never have thought of advertising but for you," said Kate, resentfully.

"Probably not!" retorted Mrs. Leslie, tartly. "But now he will do it, and quickly, if he is sensible."

Mrs. Leslie was wrong. The Doctor did not advertise for a governess, although when he left he was firmly resolved upon doing so. He drove home quickly to his handsome house in Canonbury, and enjoyed an excellent dinner by the bright fire in his comfortable dining-room, with a renewed appreciation of the excellent Mrs. Jessop. Then he summoned that lady in his presence, and with very little circumlocution broke to her the news of the promised invasion and the suggested panacea. Finding that Mrs. Jessop took the matter on the whole amiably, he felt considerably relieved in mind, and began placidly to smoke his pipe over the Times. The leading article was stupid, soporific, the tobacco soothing, the fire hot; he was just hovering in delicious languor upon the very borders of dreamland when a knock at the door roused him abruptly. Of course, he was called out.

Had the call been from a well-to-do patient who fostered a half-fancied illness, he might have been more put out than he certainly was when, upon turning into the street, he felt the keen east wind nipping his ears; but it was from a poor house lying in the midst of a very labyrinth of squalid back streets and foul courts, and yet but a mere stone's-throw from his own comfortable dwelling.

The Doctor did all that he could for the patient—a disheveled woman, who had fallen, while drunk, and cut her head. He bound up the wound, gave a prescription; and, leaving directions with the voluble Irish charwoman who filled the place of nurse, left the close, evil-smelling room, glad to breathe even the tainted air outside, and as quickly as he could retraced his steps.

He had left the last of the wretched narrow streets behind him, and was turning into a wider road which led by a short cut to the adjacent thoroughfare, when he heard a shriek—a terrible cry of agony or fear—perhaps both—and there, not more than a hundred yards before him, standing out black against the surrounding gray, two figures were frantically struggling—a man and a woman.

George Brudenell, slight and wiry in figure, was active and swift as a boy. He shouted and ran, but, before he could reach the two, the man had violently wrested his arm free and raised it in the air. There was a flash of steel as it descended, a shrill cry that broke off into a moan; and the Doctor, hardly able to check himself, almost stumbled over the woman as she fell at his feet.

CHAPTER II.

Doctor Brudenell's first rapid glance about him as he recovered his balance assured him that pursuit would be futile. The man had darted off down a narrow turning which had led into a maze of streets. Already his rapid footsteps had ceased to echo on the pavement; he was lost by this time in the busy restless throng of Saturday night foot-passengers. The Doctor, abandoning any idea of chasing and securing him, lost not a moment in doing what he could. The short street was a new one, having on one side a neglected piece of waste land, where bricks, gravel, and mortar were flung in confusion; upon the other a row of half-finished houses. A curve at its upper end hid the thoroughfare beyond, although the sound of wheels and the hoarse cries of hucksters were audible to him as he dropped upon one knee, and gently raised the inert figure. Blood was upon it; he felt it and knew that it was staining his hand. Had no one heard that dreadful, thrilling cry but himself? It seemed not. He shouted loudly with the full power of his lungs:

"Help, help! Murder! Here—help!"

He was heard, for, as he loudly shouted again, voices answered him; and in a few moments a group of men and women had gathered about him, eager, excited, questioning. Before he could answer them they made way for a sergeant of police whom Doctor Brudenell happened to know. He explained hastily; the knot commented; the sergeant was cool and professional.

"Pity you weren't quick enough to nab him, sir!"

He went down upon his knee and turned the light of his lantern upon the ghastly face.

"H'm! Young, and a spanker to look at, I should say! Wonder if it was robbery? Is she dead, sir?"

"No." The Doctor laid her gently down, his practiced hand over the heart. "No; she's not dead. The blow was aimed at her heart, but something in her dress—a corset, probably—turned the weapon aside. Call me a cab, somebody. You're off duty, I think, sergeant—can you come with me?"

"I am, sir. Always happens so when there's anything doing," muttered the sergeant, discontentedly. "Here's another of our people that ain't, though," as a second sergeant forced his way through the group, followed by a constable. "Baxter, you'd best step round and report this little job, and not lose any time about it, either. It's attempted murder—that's what the game is. Chap made off as if he'd got springs in his heels."

The second officer bent down as the first had done, glanced at the bloodless face, asked a question or two, and started off at a smart pace, the fringe of the crowd hurrying after him.

The Doctor looked at his companion, repeating:

"Can you come with me? I may want assistance."

"With pleasure, sir! You'll take her to the hospital, I suppose?"

"No. My house is nearer; and, unless the wound is looked to at once, I don't answer for the consequences. There is no objection, I suppose?"

The sergeant thought there could be no objection, although the hospital was "the usual thing." The Doctor put aside that consideration contemptuously. From what he could see of the wound, he was prepared to state professionally that any delay would be highly dangerous. The sergeant yielded the point respectfully, but protestingly; and the cab came, bringing an excited crowd in its train.

There was no lack of proffered help; but the Doctor and the sergeant lifted the insensible woman into the cab between them. On arriving at the Doctor's house the two men carried her indoors; then bells rang, maid-servants hurried, exclaimed, and questioned; and soon the door of the library was closed upon all except Mrs. Jessop and the Doctor. The sergeant retired to the dining-room, and meditatively took an inventory of its furniture and appointments, as he awaited further developments. Noticing the Doctor's decanter of choice old port, which was still upon the table where he had left it, the officer helped himself to a glassful, drinking it with evident relish.

Half an hour passed before the Doctor entered. He took his seat thoughtfully by the fire, and motioned to the sergeant to draw his chair nearer.

"The wound is not much—merely a deep flesh-wound," he observed, abruptly.

"Glad to hear it, I'm sure," returned the sergeant, politely.

"She has lost a great deal of blood, will be much weakened, and is totally insensible now," Doctor Brudenell continued; "but no vital part is touched—not the fault of that scoundrel, though, sergeant."

"Ah!" replied the sergeant, intelligently.

The Doctor had motioned to him to help himself to the wine, and he did so now with contemplative deliberation.

"Then you think it is a case of intended murder, I take it, sir?"

"As far as my judgment serves me—yes. I should say the blow was meant to kill her—indeed, only the steel of her corset saved her."

"H'm, I thought as much! Now, as to motive, sir; have you got any theory?"

"Robbery, I suppose. Ah"—as the sergeant shook his head with a wise air—"you don't think so, then!"

"No, I don't, sir. Maybe, of course, but I doubt it. A man don't use a knife when his fists will do, as a rule. And look you here, sir," said the sergeant, leaning forward to place his broad hand for a moment upon the Doctor's knee—"when you find a fine old gentleman with a bald crown or a 'spectable old lady with a bag and umbrella, tipped over neat in a corner, you may put it down to robbery; for you won't find anything in their pockets, I'll wager. But you find a good-looking fellow with a ha'porth of rat poison inside of him that he didn't put there himself, or a young woman stabbed that's as handsome as that one"—jerking his head toward the door—"and you won't go far wrong if you put it down to jealousy."

The Doctor sat silently pondering. The sergeant slowly filled his glass again.

"You've examined her dress, of course, sir? Anything in the pockets?"

"Nothing—absolutely nothing!"

"Nothing torn? No appearance of having been robbed?"

"No. Merely the cut where the blow was given."

"Just so, sir. About the weapon—an ordinary knife, should you say?"

"No; from the appearance and general character of the wound it was caused by a two-edged blade."

"H'm! Sort of dagger—stiletto kind of thing?" queried the sergeant.

"I should say so."

The sergeant gave a prolonged whistle, with an air of intense satisfaction.

"Supports my idea, you see, sir. A man going about with a dagger in his pocket usually means to use it. A case of jealousy—that's what it is! It's surprising, I'm sure, the way a man will put his neck into a rope if there's a woman t'other side of it. You wait till this young woman comes round, and you'll find that that's about the size of it.

The work of some hot-headed young fool she's thrown over, I expect; or, maybe, she's bolted from her husband, and it's a case of elopement. Shouldn't wonder, for the handsomer they are the more mischief they get up to. That's my experience."

"I hope you are mistaken," said the Doctor, rising and looking thoughtfully at the fire. "I hope you are, but we shall see. Fill your glass, sergeant!"

"Thank you, sir, I am sure." The sergeant obediently filled his glass for the fourth time, and held it critically between his eye and the light. "Well, we shall see, as you say. When do you fancy you'll be able to speak to her, may I ask?"

"Impossible to say. She may be sensible to-morrow, or the shock may cause a fever, in which case her condition may become highly dangerous. I can't possibly say."

"Pity there isn't something about her by which she might be identified," mused the sergeant, thoughtfully. "But it'll all be in the papers to-morrow, and it will be odd if it doesn't catch the eye of some one who knows her. But she's French, if I don't mistake, or at any rate, not English."

Doctor Brudenell, recalling his impression of the ghastly face as he had seen it, first in the light of the sergeant's lantern, and afterward lying upon a pillow hardly whiter than itself, silently endorsed this opinion. No, decidedly she was not English; but he did not think she was French. The sergeant thoughtfully emptied his glass, and set it down upon the table.

"We'll do all we can, of course, but it strikes me that the chances of nabbing the man don't amount to much unless the young man comes to herself in time to help us. And, if she does, it's about twenty to one that she puts us on a wrong scent. Well, I'm on duty again directly, and I'll be going. Will you step down to the station with me, sir?"

"Certainly, if you think it necessary."

The sergeant thought that "it might be as well," and the Doctor put on his hat and coat, and walked with his companion to the police-station, where the inspector on duty, who had received one report already, listened to his statement, wrote it all down imperturbably, and approved with some warmth of the sergeant's theory as to "jealousy." Fists or a knuckle-duster did well enough for robbery, the inspector observed oracularly; it was only when a man went "a bit off his head" that he took to daggers; and there was more of that sort of thing about—presumably meaning jealousy—than any one would credit. Though, when it came to going it to that extent, the inspector's private opinion was that no woman was worth it.

"Is there much chance of capturing this man, do you think?" Doctor Brudenell asked.

Why, that depended. If the young woman came to herself—say to-morrow—and told the truth, you would know where you were; but if, on the other hand, the young woman chose to put them on an altogether false scent—which was rather more likely than not—why, where would they be?

Feeling that he could not successfully answer this official poser, the Doctor bade the sergeant and the inspector good-night, and, repeating his former assurances of perfect willingness to do whatever he could in the affair, walked out of the police-station. At home, by the dining-room fire, he found the invaluable Mrs. Jessop waiting for him.

"Well, Mrs. Jessop, and how is our patient now?" he inquired, cheerfully.

He did not feel cheerful, but Mrs. Jessop had shown some slight reluctance and resentment at being suddenly called upon to assume the function of nurse to a totally unknown and much too handsome young woman, and he thought it only prudent to conciliate her.

"Pretty much the same, sir—hasn't stirred so much as a finger or opened her eyes; though whether or not it's a natural sleep I couldn't take upon myself to say."

"I'll step up-stairs again with you in a moment. What I fear is fever, consequent on the shock. If we can keep off that, she will most likely awaken sensible enough. I hope so, I am sure, for the sake of catching that cowardly villain, whoever he was."

"He must have meant to murder her, you think, sir?" inquired Mrs. Jessop, smoothing her cap-ribbons, thoughtfully.

"I am afraid so. Poor girl! She is quite young?"

"Yes, sir."

"And most remarkably handsome?"

"No doubt, sir."

"She is a foreigner, I fancy. It is most unfortunate that there is nothing on her by which we can identify her. By the way—I did not notice—did you see if she wore rings?"

"No, sir."

"Not a wedding-ring?"—"No, sir."

"And not a trinket of any kind about her?"

"Not one, sir."

"Nothing whatever?" persisted the Doctor musingly, as he held out his hands to the fire. They were cold, for the February night air was keen.

"There was this, sir," said Mrs. Jessop, abruptly.

She held out to him upon the palm of her plump hand a tiny roll of paper, tied with a wisp of faded red silk.

"Where did you find this?"

"In a little pocket inside the bosom of her gown, sir—it looked as if it had been made for it."

"Have you read it?"—"No, sir. It's gibberish."

The Doctor untied and unrolled the little packet, then looked at it by the gaslight. It was covered with characters of a deep red color, curious and fantastic, and to him absolutely meaningless. It looked strange, uncanny, witch-like. Was it a charm? The Doctor studied it wonderingly for a few moments, and then laughed at the thought of such an absurd fancy assailing him! He rolled up and re-tied the little packet.

"Well, that won't help us much," he said. "As I thought, we must wait for light from her, poor girl. Take care of it, Mrs. Jessop; she may attach some fanciful value to it."

Doctor Brudenell, standing by the bed in the comfortable room, to which the unknown woman had been carried, looked down at her curiously and scrutinizingly. Upon the white pillows he saw a pale face lying—a face that was exquisitely chiseled, the head crowned by a wonderful mass of thick black hair.

"Beautiful!" he muttered, under his breath, and turning away. "I should fancy it was jealousy!"

The next day's papers contained a sufficiently thrilling account of the attempted murder of a lady in Rockmore Street; but, although an elaborate description of the victim's person and attire was given and enlarged upon with due journalistic skill, it brought no anxious troop of friends and relatives to inquire at Doctor Brudenell's door; and the best efforts of the inspector and his subordinates to track the would-be murderer came to ignominious grief, for the only person who could perchance have put them upon his track lay tossing in the delirium of fever.

CHAPTER III.

"Hang the brats!" exclaimed Dr. Brudenell, angrily. "If this goes on for long they'll drive me mad, I swear!"

He was annoyed, chafed, irritated, more out of temper than he had ever been before. The preceding week had been to him a period of purgatory; the calm of his house was broken; his study was no longer a sanctuary; the maids were flurried; Mrs. Jessop spoiled the soup. The bachelor, transformed suddenly into a family-man without any preliminary steps, was amazed and bewildered; the sufferings of his married acquaintances filled him with a grotesque feeling of pity, with the sincerest sympathy. He especially commiserated Laura's husband—for the three children had turned out to be three emphatic editions of Laura—with additions.

Just now the uproar which had caused the master of the house to spring up from his dinner was more than usually vociferous. The three had escaped from their extemporized nursery, and had shouted and tumbled tumultuously down the staircase and into the hall. The street door happened to be open, and the consequences were disastrous. One rushed down the steps with a scream of triumph, which changed into a shrill shriek of anger as he was pursued, captured, and brought back by Patrick, in spite of violent kicking and struggling; another, backing unconsciously toward the kitchen staircase, overbalanced, and, descending with a succession of startling bumps, fell into a tray of glasses with a terrific crash; while the third and youngest, not precisely comprehending what was the matter, but being of a highly sympathetic temperament, threw herself upon the devoted Patrick, screaming, kicking, and scratching furiously; which, added to the shouts of the youth whom Patrick carried upside down, and the wails of the unfortunate whom Mrs. Jessop had just rescued from the *débris* of the glasses, swelled the uproar into a chorus that was almost deafening.

The Doctor sat down again, and took up his knife and fork with an energy which sent the gravy flying over the snowy cloth.

"Confound the little wretches! I'll advertise to-morrow!" he said.

The noise outside subsided a little as Mrs. Jessop appeared upon the scene, but the next moment it broke out again, growing louder as the staircase was mounted. Evidently Mrs. Jessop intended to put the rebels to bed—a resolution which did not apparently please them, for Doctor Brudenell distinctly heard his elder nephew threaten to punch the head of that worthy woman, while his brother and sister appeared to be trying to dance upon her toes. Then came a cessation of the hubbub, sudden and soothing, and the Doctor finished his dinner in peace.

Crossing the hall toward his study a little later, with the intention of getting a book to add to the enjoyment of a very fine-flavored cigar, he encountered Mrs. Jessop, somewhat flushed and tumbled, coming down-stairs, and stopped to speak to her.

"Well, Mrs. Jessop, got rid of your charges for to-night—eh?" he said, good-humoredly.

"That I haven't, sir, for to go to bed they wouldn't! I've seen a good many children, but never did I see children so set upon their own way as them children!" declared Mrs. Jessop, emphatically.

The Doctor felt that this was correct; his opinion being that any children in the least degree resembling Laura's luckily did not exist anywhere.

"Oh, spoilt, Mrs. Jessop," he remarked, judicially—"spoilt—that's it! They'll be better, you'll find, when we get a good strict governess for them; and that reminds me, I must certainly advertise for one to-morrow. I don't know how it is that it has slipped my memory for so long. So they're not in bed, the young rogues—eh?"

"No, sir—they're with Miss Boucheafen."

"With her? You should not have allowed it—you should not have let them go in?" said the Doctor, quickly and peremptorily.

"I couldn't help it, sir," returned the housekeeper, stolidly. "They started making such a racket of stamping and screaming outside her door that she heard and opened it to ask what was the matter. Of course, they were for rushing in before I could keep them back, and so she said, Let them stay awhile, and she would keep them still; and so there they are, and she telling them some fairy-tale nonsense."

"Well, well!" exclaimed the Doctor; and then added, "How does Miss Boucheafen seem to-day?"

"Better, I think, sir—she seems so. She asked me to say that if you were at liberty she would be glad if you could spare her a few minutes."

"Tell her I will come up presently," said Doctor Brudenell, going on to the study. "Don't let those young torments stay there long enough to tire her, Mrs. Jessop, if you please. She is still very weak."

But, when he went up-stairs half an hour later, he found that Mrs. Jessop had not yet succeeded in getting the "young torments" out of Miss Boucheafen's room. Miss Boucheafen was sitting in a great chair by the fire, her dark hair streaming over her shoulders, and with the children grouped about her—Floss on her knee, Maggie perched on the arm of her chair, and Tom kneeling at her feet, all three listening intently to what she was telling them. What it was the Doctor did not hear, for the group broke up at his entrance; Tom sprang to his feet, Maggie jumped down, and Miss Boucheafen let Floss slip from her knees to the floor.

"Oh, uncle, I wish you hadn't come!" cried Tom.

"It was such a yuvly 'tory!" lamented Maggie, whose five-year-old vocabulary was but limited; while Floss, whose name was short for Ferdinand, and who had perhaps not yet fully recovered from the shock of his tumble down the kitchen stairs, contented himself with surveying his relative with an implacable expression as he sucked his thumb.

"I will finish the story to-morrow, perhaps," said Miss Boucheafen, quietly; "go to bed now. See—Mrs. Jessop is waiting for you."

They went without a murmur—indeed, they hardly looked sulky, but walked off in the wake of Mrs. Jessop, very unlike Laura's children, the Doctor thought. He was amazed, and stood for a few moments, after the door had closed behind them, quite silent, and looking at Alexia Boucheafen.

A month had passed since the night of the attempted murder in Rockmore Street, and, although during that time she had lived under his roof, George Brudenell knew no more of this girl than her name. One thing, however, he did know, and was growing to know better day by day—that she was beautiful, with a beauty that was to him unique, startling; he had seen none like it before. She had risen as the children left the room, and stood with her hand resting upon the mantel-shelf, her eyes gazing downward at the fire, her head above the level of his. He looked at her, thinking how beautiful she was, and thinking—not for the first time either—that he was not sure whether that very beauty did not repel rather than charm him. For it seemed to have at once the glitter of ice and the hardness of stone; her large, dark, bright eyes seemed to pierce him, but they never touched his heart; a smile sometimes broke the perfect lines of her lips, but never reached those eyes; the natural play of her features seemed to be checked; she appeared to be as incapable of tears as of laughter, of grief as of joy; no rush of warm blood ever tinted the strange pallor of her cheeks with crimson; her voice was rich and full, but there was a jarring note in its melancholy music; the girl was like marble—breathing, moving, living, but marble still.

The Doctor waited for her to speak; but, either from perversity or indifference, she stood like a statue, and would not even raise her eyes. He was forced to break the silence, which embarrassed him, and he knew that he spoke awkwardly.

"I think," he said, "that you wished to speak to me?"

"Yes, sir, if you please."

This was another anomaly—her words were always of a meek and submissive character, but her voice, her look, her gestures were those of a queen. The Doctor felt this, but hardly its incongruity, as she slowly resumed her seat and signed to him to be seated also.

"I am quite at your service, of course," he replied, as he sat down; "but first let me ask how you are feeling?"

"I am well," she answered, gravely. "A little weak, still, perhaps, but it will pass. I wish—ah, pardon me, I am forgetting that I am not to thank you, sir!"

She had attempted to thank him before, when she first recovered her senses and realized her position, but he had sensitively deprecated that. On that same day she had told him her name, told him that she was French, that in England she was friendless, and that of what little she possessed she had been robbed by the man whom he had seen attack her—a man whom she had never seen before; and this was all that he knew about her. He wanted to know more, but he sat before her wondering how to phrase his questions. In spite of his curiosity he would have deferred them had it been possible, but it was not possible; and he broke the silence timidly, for as he spoke she looked at him full in the face with her dark eyes.

"Miss Boucheafen, if you are strong enough to allow of it—"

"As I said, sir, I am well."

"I must, with your permission, ask you a few questions." He hesitated, almost confused under her steady gaze. "I am presuming that you would rather reply to me than be questioned by a police-officer?"

"I do prefer it, sir."

"Then," said the Doctor, "this man who so murderously attacked you—you can tell nothing about him?"

"Nothing, sir—I know nothing."

"Absolutely nothing?"

"Absolutely!"

"You do not know his motive?"

"Ah, sir—you forget! He robbed me."

"True, true!" the Doctor returned, a slight flush tinting his cheeks, for he fancied that he detected a mocking gleam in her eyes, a suspicion of a smile curving her lips.

"True—I had forgotten. Pray pardon me," he said, "but the attack was so violent, the blow so savage, the weapon must have been so keen, that it is almost impossible to connect it with a mere attempt to commit a paltry robbery. I thought, and the police thought, that it was a case of intended murder."

"Ah, sir, they are clever, your police, but they sometimes make mistakes! Is it not so?"

Doctor Brudenell's face flushed crimson. Was she laughing at him? It looked like it. He was taken aback, discomfited. He did not know how to go on, but she gave him no chance, for she spoke herself, emphasizing her words by rapid gestures and much energetic waving of her white hands.

"Listen, then, sir. This is all I know—that this man followed me—why, I have no idea—that he came upon me suddenly in the solitary street and asked me for money; that, when I refused it, he tore my purse away; that, as I seized his arm and screamed, he wrenched it free, and struck me with what you tell me was a dagger. I know no more but what you tell me—nothing."

George Brudenell, listening and looking, believed after all his own fancy was but a fancy. The theory of the sergeant and the inspector was only a theory, a mere empty possibility, unsupported by fact. He abandoned both ideas forthwith.

"Miss Boucheafen, could you recognize this man?"

"I think not—I am sure not." She shook her head, her eyes fixed musingly upon the fire. "It was dark. No—I could not recognize him."

"Nor could I, unfortunately."

"And yet you saw him?"

"I saw him, yes—but only well enough to know that he was young, tall and dark. And such a description would apply equally well to a hundred men within a stone's throw of the house at the present moment."

"True," admitted Alexia Boucheafen, calmly.

"Since you can give me absolutely no clue, I am afraid that the chances of capturing him, particularly after the lapse of a month, are so small as to be worth nothing."

"Less than nothing," she assented. "It would be better to abandon the endeavor."

"I am afraid that is what will have to be done, from sheer lack of ground to work upon. But it is horrible," said the Doctor, rising with an unusual display of excitement—"absolutely horrible to think of this scoundrel's going scot free! It is abominable that such things should be possible in the heart of a great city such as this!"

A smile parted the girl's lips, but it did not light up her drooping eyes. The smile seemed to imply that such a city held secret stranger things than that. Doctor Brudenell did not see the smile; he was a clever man, but it would have been far beyond his fathoming if he had seen it. He returned to his chair and sat down again.

"In asking my questions, Miss Boucheafen, I have forgotten yours. I assume that you wished to ask me some."

"Yes." She looked straight into his eyes again, and her slender hands were clasped firmly together; he fancied he detected an expression of doubt and anxiety in her glance. "Sir, I have said that I am almost strong—you know that I am so. It follows, then, that I shall be able soon to leave here."

Yes, it certainly followed that such an event would take place—the Doctor acknowledged it, but at the very thought he experienced a strange sense of loss. She was so young, so beautiful, so friendless. Where would she go? What would she do? He was silent, and waited for her to continue speaking. It seemed that she drew courage from his look, for, after she had glanced at him with eager scrutiny, she went on abruptly:

"I shall be able to leave, but I do not desire it. I am alone, I am friendless, penniless. Doctor Brudenell, I beg you, let me remain!"

"Remain?" he echoed in bewilderment.

"Yes. Why should I not? I have been a governess; it was to be a governess that I came to this England of yours—it is a governess that you require for the children, your nephews and niece— Your housekeeper told me so but a little while ago. I should be industrious; I could teach them well. Suffer me, then, to remain."

The Doctor hesitated, feeling uneasy, astonished, puzzled. Did she mean it? Did she fully realize what she was doing—she, young, beautiful, talented—in pleading to be tied down to the dull routine of a nursery-governess? Did she remember that beneath his roof her position might be questioned by carping feminine tongues? He remembered it—not for his own sake, but for hers; but he only answered, overcoming his first feeling of surprise:

"But my dear young lady, you must be perfectly aware that your attainments are far beyond those required for the teaching of such young children as these."

"Ah, sir, yes! But are beggars then choosers?"

Doctor Brudenell got up, walked to the window and back again.

"It is a fact," he said, slowly, "that in London you have no friends?"

"Yourself," she replied.

"And beyond?"

"Not one."

"Then, until you wish to leave, or until some more suitable and congenial sphere of work is opened for you, remain, my child."

George Brudenell, speaking thus, had forgotten her beauty, her queen-like dignity, and remembered only her youth and helplessness. He went down-stairs with an odd feeling, thinking how quickly, with what almost disconcerting rapidity, she had, after her point was gained, recovered that icy composure of manner; remembering, too, how cold and lifeless her hand had lain in his when she gave it in saying good-night. But he was glad that she was going to stay; he had that curious sense of relief from tension which is the result of anxiety removed, as though to protect her, to befriend and keep her safe, were an object which had long lain near his heart. He was a little astonished, but he explained his feeling to himself. She was too young and far too beautiful to live friendless in the modern Babylon called London.

He rang for Mrs. Jessop, and explained to that excellent woman this new phase of affairs. Mrs. Jessop, respectfully listening, received the news in a manner which could hardly be termed gracious, but prudently gave but small expression to her opinions. Mrs. Jessop's situation in the Doctor's household was a very comfortable one, and she did not desire to lose it; but Mrs. Jessop's eyes were as keen as those of most women, a fact which she often insisted upon when talking to various confidential friends—so keen, indeed, that they sometimes descried things which did not exist. At present, however, Mrs. Jessop merely told herself that, if Miss Boucheafen had not been quite so handsome, her chance of remaining in her present quarters would not have been by any means so great.

Mrs. Jessop, having formed this astute conviction, walked out of the dining-room, and went down to her snug sitting-room, where, sitting down by the fire, she fell to darning a table-cloth while she thought things over. She had arrived at a conclusion that would have astonished her master, and she chanced to want more cotton, and rose to get it from her work-box. And among the reels and hanks of tape she saw something that astonished her.

"I declare," said Mrs. Jessop to herself, "if I haven't forgot to give it to her after all!"

"It" was the only thing which had been found upon Alexia Boucheafen, the tiny roll of paper, covered with its grotesque red characters and tied with its piece of faded silk. Rather ashamed of her forgetfulness and neglect, the housekeeper took it and went up-stairs at once to the new governess's room.

Alexia was sitting by the fire, almost as Doctor Brudenell had left her, her chin drooping upon her hands, her face almost hidden by her hair. She started at Mrs. Jessop's entrance, flung back the black tresses, and looked up.

"What is it?"

"I'm sure I'm very sorry, miss," Mrs. Jessop faltered, finding herself forced into somewhat reluctant respect before the bright gaze of the imperious eyes, "and I hope you'll excuse my forgetfulness. I quite forgot until just this moment to give you this."

For a moment the girl stared languidly at the extended hand, then with a cry sprang suddenly from her chair, seized the little packet, and pressed it passionately to her lips and to her breast.

"Ah," she cried, "he did not take it—he did not take it—he did not take it"—incoherently repeating the words and redoubling her strange caresses.

"Take it, miss!" exclaimed the astonished Mrs. Jessop. "Why, what should he want to take it for, the murdering villain? And how could he take it, seeing that it was fast inside the bosom of your gown?"

"Go!" cried Alexia, pointing to the door with an imperious gesture. "Leave me to myself!"

The housekeeper went with the impression that Miss Boucheafen had fallen upon her knees beside her chair, and that she was sobbing harsh suffocating sobs beneath the shining veil of her streaming hair.

Peace returned to the Doctor's household; the children were calmed, manageable; they stood in awe of their governess, but they liked her; in the staid Canonbury house Miss

Boucheafen was popular. Her name was the only stumbling-block. Her pupils could not pronounce it, the servants blundered over it, and Mrs. Jessop declared it "heathenish." By slow degrees it was dropped, and she became merely "Mademoiselle."

CHAPTER IV.

"Children," said Miss Boucheafen, abruptly, "you have been good to-day, and it is fine. We will go out."

The children, engaged in turning their nursery into a very fair imitation of Pandemonium and in driving the unhappy nursemaid nearly mad, stopped their various operations at these words from their governess as she entered, and stared at her—partly perhaps because they were not conscious of having been less troublesome than they usually were, but more because of her last sentence. Did Mademoiselle really say, "We will go out?" She had been their governess for six weeks now, and during all that time had not once been outside the street door.

"Do you mean you'll take us?" cried Tom, the eldest and the readiest-tongued.

"Shan't go with Ellen, I shan't!" muttered Floss, sulkily.

"Nasty Ellen—won't go with Ellen!" whimpered Maggie, with a thumb in her mouth.

"You will all go with me and Ellen," said Alexia, quietly, beginning with her deft fingers to remove grubby pinafores and brush tumbled hair. "Will you get ready, Ellen? And do not waste time, please, or we shall lose the best part of the afternoon."

Ellen departed willingly. She was not sure that she liked Mademoiselle, but there was no doubt that she intensely detested her daily task of taking the three "troublesome brats" for their walk. If Mademoiselle liked to try it—well, Ellen only breathed a fervent wish that she might like it—"that's all!"

Miss Boucheafen, making great haste over the toilet of her pupils, had them ready and was ready herself before Ellen, and filled up the spare time by pacing the hall from end to end as she waited. Not hastily—the perfect grace of her every motion was too complete for haste—not even impatiently, for the set expression of her face never changed, and no flush of excitement tinted the ivory pallor of her cheeks. If her eyes were a little brighter, a little wider open than usual, it was very little. Mrs. Jessop, passing through the hall as the governess and pupils waited, confessed to herself, with reluctant honesty, as she looked at the stately young figure in its plain dark dress, that there was no denying that "Ma'm'selle" did look like a queen.

It was the beginning of May, and, for a wonder, hot and bright enough almost for July; the afternoon sun shone down warm and brilliant. As Alexia stepped out into its glare, she stopped and almost staggered, putting her hand to her throat, while she shivered violently. The round-eyed maid, watching, was quite sympathetic. No wonder she felt odd, poor young lady, remembering what had happened to her the last time she was out!

"Where shall we go?" demanded Tom, tugging at Alexia's hand.

"Want to go an' see Mrs. Yeslie," murmured Maggie.

"I'm going to look at the shops," declared Floss with emphasis. "I can spend my shilling if I want to, Uncle George said!"

"No, no—not to-day," demurred the governess, quickly. "Listen, children. The shops you can see any day—to-morrow, perhaps; but to-day we will go somewhere else."

"Where else?" demanded Floss, critically, with a fond look at the shilling which he had drawn out of his knickerbocker pocket.

"Into the park," said Alexia. "We will all ride there in a tram-car. You will like that?"

"Finsbury Park?" questioned Tom. "Oh, all right! I don't mind. Only, I say, let's go up to the water where the ducks are!"

"Yes—let's," added Floss, restoring the shilling to his pocket.

"Want's some buns to feed 'em wiv, poor fings," murmured Maggie, with pathetic intonation.

"Yes, you shall go [to] the water and have the buns," said Alexia. She had been walking rapidly all this time—almost too rapidly for the little feet trotting beside her—and did not pause or speak until they reached Highbury Corner, which was more crowded and busy than usual this warm afternoon. A tram-car was waiting, and she hurried her charges into it, taking no heed of Tom's desire to sit where he could see the horses, or of Floss's loudly-expressed determination to ride on the roof. She took her seat, and, leaning back, drew her black gossamer veil tightly over her face, and closed her eyes, seeming to become totally oblivious of her surroundings.

Ellen, sitting with Maggie on her knee, distracted by Tom's ceaseless questions upon the one side and by Floss's incessant demands to be put out on the roof upon the other, felt a little sulky and injured. Really it was too bad of mademoiselle! If she came out with the children she might at least take her share in amusing and keeping them quiet. Ellen, at any rate, was not sorry when the park-gates were reached. A plentiful supply of buns was procured, and the children, with shrill screams and whoops of delight, started off for the ducks and the water.

"Oh, dear," cried the nursemaid, quite dismayed at suddenly finding herself alone with the governess, "they'll lose themselves, Ma'm'selle! There's such a many other children about we shall never find 'em."

"Keep them in sight, then," said Alexia. "Follow them, Ellen. You had better not wait for me. My head aches, and I cannot walk fast."

"But we shall lose you, too, Ma'm'selle," demurred the girl, hesitatingly.

"No, no; I will follow you slowly. Go; they may fall into the water if you linger."

"Miss Maggie's nigh sure to, with they buns!" said the girl, taking the alarm, and without any more loitering she darted after the runaways.

Alexia did not follow. For a moment she stood on the broad gravel walk looking about her. Groups of figures were scattered about the smooth turf—young ladies with novels; old ladies with crochet and poodles; nurse- [here a lack in the original text] The girl looked, not at, but around and beyond them; her great eyes seemed to be searching, as if surprised at not seeing something, and yet dreading to see it. Then their expression changed; for a moment her figure swayed; the next she was walking gracefully, slowly, languidly, toward a rustic seat which stood upon the smooth greensward in a somewhat lonely spot. It stood at an angle formed by two flower-beds, and was backed by a clump of shrubbery. Upon it there was one figure seated—that of a man.

The governess approached this figure slowly. A middle-aged man, loosely-dressed, hair turning gray, dark-complexioned, with a scar on his cheek, a scar such as a slash with a keen-edged knife might have made. She approached and passed him; she did not look at him; he did not look at her; he appeared to be quite absorbed in absently cutting and fashioning a rough stick with the aid of a large clasp-knife. He gazed before him abstractedly, brushed the splinters of wood from his knee, and laid the knife down upon the seat beside him, the edge of the blade uppermost. The girl shuddered; the ivory pallor of her cheeks grew gray beneath her veil. She passed on round the clump of bushes and returned. The man had abandoned his whittling, and, with his chin upon his hand, whistled as he looked down at the grass at his feet. His right hand played absently with the open knife; now the edge was upward, now downward, now he half closed it, then opened it wide again. Alexia Boucheafen's breath came rapidly; one violent throb of her heart almost suffocated her; but, graceful, upright, stately, she passed the seat as though it were vacant; she did not appear to glance at the man sitting there, toying with the knife, and whistling under his breath. She passed him, and, as she did so, her gloved hand made a swift motion, and a white object gleamed upon the turf behind her. A paper had fluttered from her fingers, and lay close to the rustic seat.

Tom, Floss, and Maggie, flinging pieces of bun to voracious ducks, were delighted—far too absorbed to remember their governess; and Ellen, finding herself fully occupied in keeping their hats on their heads and themselves outside the railings that surrounded the lake, had also forgotten Miss Boucheafen completely. The girl was quite startled when she saw the tall dark figure suddenly beside her, the great bright eyes shining through the black veil. And how pale she was—her cheeks were quite white!

"Lor, Ma'm'selle," she cried, with loud-voiced sympathy, "how bad you do look!"

"I'm tired," said Alexia abruptly. "Children, are you ready to go?"

"Ready? Why, we ain't had half a walk!" demurred Tom.

"I'm hungry!" exclaimed Floss, tugging at Miss Boucheafen's gown. "Maggie went an' threw all the buns to the ducks, she did—little stupid."

"You 'tory, I never! You eatened two yourself, you did," Maggie declared indignantly. "You's a geedy boy—a dedful geedy boy! Isn't he a geedy boy, Ma'm'selle?"

"Never mind, we will get more buns as we go out," said Alexia. "Come now, children. I am tired—my head aches. We will come some other time—to-morrow perhaps—and stay longer. Come now."

They walked away from the water, and gained the broad path leading to the gates. Alexia slackened her pace, and, releasing Floss's hand, but still retaining Maggie's, fell slightly behind, sauntering slowly, playing with the buttons of her cloak, keeping her eyes fixed straight before her. They were passing a seat close to the edge of the path, upon which a man was sitting—a middle-aged, loose-jointed man with gray hair. A bright object lay at his feet—a small ball of gorgeous tints; the child saw it, uttered a delighted cry, and struggled to release her hand. It was released and she started to pick up the prize. It was hardly in her grasp when she screamed out, frightened, for the man with the gray hair had taken hold of her arm, and was speaking to her, not roughly, although his voice was harsh and stern.

"My little one—see, the lady has dropped this paper. Give it to her; and as for this bauble, take it. Go!"

He released her. The child was scared, but she held in one hand the paper he had given to her, in the other the gay-colored ball. He pointed peremptorily after the tall retreating figure of Alexia Boucheafen, and, frightened at his frowning face, the child darted toward "Ma'm'selle."

"Ma'm'selle, Ma'm'selle!" She tugged at the governess's dress, at her hand. "'Ook what he dave me!"—holding up the ball. "Nice, nice man, vewy nice! Floss s'an't have it, he s'ant—Floss a geedy boy. He dived it me for meself. Oh, an' yes!"

With a sudden remembrance of something less absorbing than the ball, she held up the paper—a mere folded scrap. Alexia seized it eagerly, held it fast in her hands, asked almost inaudibly:

"Who gave it to you, child?"

"Him did. You droppened it. Him," said the child, turning round to point. Then she cried out blankly, "Oh, him's gone!"

Miss Boucheafen glanced behind her hastily. The seat by which the gay-colored ball had lain was empty. She opened the paper, and read within it, written in a blood-red color, the one word "Absolved!"

Doctor Brudenell found his nephews and niece unusually excited and talkative when, as was his custom, he came up after his dinner to see them in Miss Boucheafen's pleasant sitting-room. The rides in the tram-cars, the park, the buns, and the ducks were enlarged upon in turn; and then Maggie produced her ball, and plunged onto such broken and lavish praises of the "vewy nice man" that the Doctor looked at the governess for enlightenment.

"A gentleman in the park, sir, gave her the ball," explained Miss Boucheafen gravely.

"And zou a letter!" cried Maggie.

"And also returned me a paper that I had dropped," amended Alexia.

"I see. Well, don't smash more windows with the ball than you can help," said the Doctor, putting his niece down upon her feet.

He rose and approached the stately young governess, standing, beautiful in the light of lamp and fire, one hand drooping at her side, the other lying upon the marble of the mantel-piece, hardly whiter and hardly colder. George Brudenell had begun to think that her coldness and gravity suited her beauty—laughter, blushes, dimples would have spoiled it. Her frigid manner did not repel him now; it had a charm for him which no warmth and graciousness could have had; and yet, perversely he longed intensely to see her both kind and sweet. How beautiful she was! He glanced at her reflected face in the mirror, and winced and frowned and bit his lip, seeing his own beside it. A small, plain, dark, clean-shaven man—he was her very antithesis.

Intellectual-looking, pleasant, refined he might perhaps claim to be considered; but how utterly, painfully unattractive he must be to her!

"I am glad to hear that you have been out, Mademoiselle," he said kindly.

"The day was so fine—it tempted me," replied Alexia.

"A very good thing; the confinement was telling upon you," resumed the Doctor. "Let me advise you to try to get out once at least every day."

"I shall do so, sir, with your permission—now."

"Now that the first plunge is taken," he remarked good-humoredly. "Well, that is wise. Do not go too far, or let these youngsters trouble you too much either out of doors or in, and you will soon feel the benefit."

"You are very good, sir," murmured the governess; "but I am quite well—indeed, quite strong."

"You must let me be the best judge of that, Mademoiselle. I am afraid you have overtaxed your strength to-day. You are looking tired."

"I am not so, indeed. Not at all too tired to play, if you desire it."

"Thank you, Mademoiselle," said the Doctor simply.

There was a piano in the room, a tolerable one; and Alexia moved slowly toward it and sat down. It had become quite an institution, this half-hour's playing which she gave the Doctor when he came up-stairs to bid the children good-night. He was disappointed if by any chance she missed it, perhaps because he hardly saw her at any other time, and because it was something to be able from his distant seat to watch her as she played. He learned her attitudes, her expressions, the poise of her head, the curve of her full throat by heart at these times.

He did not care for music, and had no knowledge of the airs she played, but he knew that he had heard no playing like hers. The magic of her fingers made the instrument speak.

Thanking her now, he did not leave the room as usual, but lingered even after the children had said good-night and gone to bed. Alexia looked at him questioningly, and he began to speak—awkwardly, as she saw, but with how much reluctance she did not suspect.

"Mademoiselle, you will pardon my recalling it. But you recollect when you first expressed a wish to remain here?"

"Yes."

She spoke quite quietly, but her eyes involuntarily widened and her lips parted. She put her hand to her bosom, felt the stiffness of paper there, and then the hand fell at her side again, and she sat looking at the fire.

"You recollect," resumed George Brudenell, with a reluctant troubled glance at her averted face, "that I told you then how perfectly aware I was that the post you wished to fill was completely below your capabilities—that in it you would be thrown away, in short—and that at the best it could only be considered as an occupation for you until something better should offer?"

"I remember, sir."

The Doctor hesitated; that "sir," with its stiffness, its cool, formal, respect, jarred upon him more and more day by day; and she hardly ever failed to use it. He was too diffident to remonstrate with a few gay words, as a more confident, easy man would have done, and chafed under it in silence.

"I am happy to tell you that something has offered."

It was a lie, and he knew it; the thought of losing her, cold and statuesque as she was to him, made him miserable, filled his heart with a keen pain—a pain which had brought very near the inevitable revelation that he was bound to make to himself. Alexia raised her head and looked at him, but she did not speak. He went on:

"It is in the family of one of my patients—not as governess, but as companion to his wife. They are wealthy, and she is a refined, cultivated, and kindhearted woman; you could, I think, hardly fail to be comfortable with her, if you care to accept the post." He paused again, but finding her still silent, went on. "That you would be upon terms of perfect equality I need not say. This lady—Mrs. Latimer— would like to see you, if you care to think further of it."

Alexia looked into his face with her great sombre eyes.

"Sir, do you then wish me to leave here?"

"Wish?" he echoed.

Was there really a sorrowful, almost reproachful, intonation in her voice? He was foolish enough to fancy so, weak enough to encourage this sudden rapid beating of his heart.

"Because, if not," she went on gently, "I would rather stay here, if I may."

"Mademoiselle, are you sure of that? Consider."

"Quite sure. I am comfortable—here it is home; you have been so kind to me! Ah, sir, do not send me away!" She spoke entreatingly, eagerly, and to herself she added, pressing her hands again upon her breast, "If he sends me from the house, I am lost."

"My child," said George Brudenell simply, again remembering only how young she was as he spoke to her thus protectingly, "stay if you wish, and as long as you wish. You shall leave only when you yourself desire it."

"I shall not do that," murmured Alexia softly; and then, having no further excuse for remaining, he went away.

The Doctor fell into a reverie before his study fire presently, and forgot the book upon his knee. He had the pleasant consciousness of an uncongenial task conscientiously performed, and without its anticipated unwelcome results being left behind. It was not an idea of his own which had caused him to inquire among his patients for a suitable situation for Alexia Boucheafen, but the hints, and then downright urgings, of his friend Mrs. Leslie. Both she and Kate Merritt had seen the governess, for in her kindness of heart the elder lady had paid more than one visit to Laura's children. Mrs. Leslie had been astonished at Alexia's beauty and stateliness, sympathetic and questioning over her story, and, upon hearing that she was to remain in the Doctor's house, had been amazed. A conventional-minded woman, with all her kindness of heart, Mrs. Leslie had been shocked. Perhaps she might not have been so had there been no scandalized and indignant influence upon her own side; but Kate had been excessively voluble upon this incipient fulfillment of her predictions, and had let her sister have very little peace indeed. Finally, Mrs. Leslie had summed up the whole case to the Doctor by assuring him that it would never do.

Well, it would have to do, he decided, when he roused himself sufficiently to know what he had been thinking about. The girl should stay if she preferred it, that was certain, in spite of all the opinions in Christendom. He rather enjoyed this outrage upon the proprieties, forgetful altogether that the same thought had been in his own mind. He was glad to know that she was tranquil and safe. Nothing more, consciously, yet.

CHAPTER V.

"Ma'm'selle, didn't you say we could go to the park again, if we were good?" said Tom, looking up from a smeary attempt to get a simple addition sum "to prove," and sucking his pencil doubtfully as he surveyed the result.

"Don't want to go to the park; want to go to the shops an' spend my shilling," exclaimed Floss, dropping a prodigious blot upon his copy of capital "B's," and instantly smearing it over the page with his arm.

"S'all go to the park, I s'all! Wants to see the ducks, pour fings, an' the nice man," cried Maggie, as usual completing the trio, and screwing up her face over the mysteries of "a, b, ab."

"Can't we go, Ma'm'selle?" demanded Tom.

"Go where?" asked Alexia. She had been leaning against the window-frame, staring out blankly. Her face was paler than usual, the lines of the mouth more rigid, her hair even more coldly absent and abstracted. Her pupils had spoken to her half a dozen times, and she had not heard them, would not have heard them now, had not Tom tugged impatiently at her gown.

"Why, to the park, as we did last week? Can't we go?"

"I don't know; we will see. Get on with your lessons now. What is that? Come in."

A tap had sounded at the door, which was now opened, and the Doctor entered. The children scrambled down from their seats and ran to him. Miss Boucheafen, turning from the window, arched her straight brows with an expression of questioning surprise. For Doctor Brudenell to appear in the school-room at that hour in the morning was an unprecedented event.

"Good-morning, Mademoiselle." He took the cold, carelessly-yielded hand into his own for a moment. "Don't let me disturb you. I simply came up to express my hope that you were not alarmed last night."

"Alarmed?" echoed Alexia.

"Then you did not hear it?"—with a look of mingled relief and astonishment. "Well, I am glad of it. But you must sleep very soundly. You were the only person in the house who was not aroused."

"I sleep very soundly." She looked at him keenly, noting that his face was drawn and that his eyes were dull, showing that he had not slept. "I did not know there was anything wrong. Not here, I hope?"

"No, not here exactly; but it is a most horrible thing." He drew a pace nearer to her, dropping his voice so that the sharp little ears that were all eagerly listening should not catch the words. "A most horrible thing. A murder, Mademoiselle!"

"A murder?" repeated Alexia.

"Nothing less; and not a hundred yards away from this door."

Miss Boucheafen had leaned back, almost fallen, against the window-frame. She was so pale that he said hastily:

"I beg your pardon—I spoke too abruptly. I have frightened you."

"No, no; I am not frightened. Go on, pray! How was it? Who was it?"

"As to who it was—a man. As to how it was, he was stabbed to the heart," answered the Doctor shortly.

"And he was found dead, and brought here?"

"Yes, at three o'clock this morning, and brought here by the police. But he was dead, and had been dead for at least half an hour. I could do nothing."

"How horrible—how very horrible!" murmured Alexia. "Did you say, sir, that he was an old man?"

"No; he is little more than a lad—a mere boy—nineteen or twenty at the most. A handsome lad too; I should fancy he was not English."

"Is there any clue as to who did it?" questioned the governess.

"Not that I know of yet. The police have had no time to work, you see," he reminded her gently.

"Ah, yes; I was forgetting, sir! Have they taken it away?"

"From here? Not yet. It must be removed to the mortuary to await the inquest, of course." He hesitated, and then added, in a voice which, in spite of all his efforts, was almost tender, "You are not afraid of its being here, are you?"

"Afraid!" A smile, as curious as fleeting, parted the beautiful lips of Alexia Boucheafen. "No, I am not afraid. I asked, because—— Sir, may I see it?"

"See it?" George Brudenell was so startled and shocked that he doubted if he had heard aright. "Surely, Mademoiselle, you do not mean what you say?"

"Yes—if I may." She spoke quite steadily and coldly. "I should like to see him—this poor murdered boy, if I may. I have never seen death, and I should like to know how it looks to be stabbed to the heart."

Surely a strange uncanny fancy in this lovely young creature! There was something morbid about it, which the Doctor did not like; it almost repelled him until he recollected how nearly this very fate had been hers. He did not like assenting, but already he was so weak with regard to her that he could refuse her nothing. So he said reluctantly:

"Come now then, if you wish."

Quite quietly, only bending her head by way of reply, she followed him out of the room and down-stairs to an apartment on a level with the hall, where the murdered man had been carried. On the threshold he stopped, looking at her doubtfully.

"Mademoiselle, are you sure of yourself? This is no sight for you."

"Yes," she answered steadily. "Pray do not fear, sir; I shall not faint. Let me see."

He stood aside and let her enter the darkened room. The blinds were drawn down, cooling liquids had been sprinkled about, there was nothing to horrify, nothing to disgust. The rigid figure, covered with white drapery, lay stretched upon the table. Without faltering, Alexia advanced, and, removing with a steady hand the cloth at the upper end, looked at the dead face thus revealed.

A boy's face, indeed, beautiful even in death, smooth-cheeked, the dark down on the delicate upper lip hardly perceptible, the black hair clustering upon the white forehead almost like a child's. The governess looked at it long and steadily, and one hand went to her bosom as she raised her eyes to the Doctor's.

"Tell me—did he suffer much?"

"No—impossible. Death must have been almost instantaneous. I doubt if he was able to cry out. Pray come away, Mademoiselle—you will faint. I should not have let you see this."

A voice in the hall called the Doctor. He was wanted, had been sent for in haste, some one was dying. He went quickly to the door to reply. Alexia Boucheafen bent down, her hand gently swept the hair from the dead boy's forehead, and for a moment her lips rested upon it.

"Poor boy," she murmured—"you were too young, too weak! It was cruel. I did my best to save you, but I could not."

"Mademoiselle, pray come," said the Doctor, turning from the door.

"I am coming, sir," replied the governess; and with that she gently replaced the sheet, and followed him quietly from the room.

Doctor Brudenell had a busy day, a day so filled with work that, coming after his sleepless night, it exhausted him. It was later than usual when he reached home, to find his dinner spoiled and Mrs. Jessop's temper ruffled. So tired was he that, when the meal was over, he fell asleep in his chair, entirely forgetting for once his regular visit to Miss Boucheafen's sitting-room to bid the children good-night. But his thoughts were all of her; and he dreamed of her as he sat—dreamed that she was in some trouble, grief, danger, of which he did not know the nature, and was helpless to relieve.

Vague as it was, the dream was to him dreadful, and the struggle that he made to find her, to save her, was so intense that he awoke—awoke to see her standing within a yard or two of his chair, a letter in her hand, the usual calmness of her face gone, her very lips unsteady. He started to his feet, and seized her hand—the dream still clung about him, and he did not realize her reality. Then he exclaimed, seeing the change in her:

"Mademoiselle, what is it? What is the matter? You are in trouble."

"Yes," she said faintly. She was trembling, and he gently induced her to sit in the chair from which he had risen. "Pray pardon me, sir," she said; "but I am troubled. I do not know what to do, and"—she faltered, glancing at him—"it seemed natural to come to you."

Sensible, practical George Brudenell was far from sensible and practical when in the presence of those glorious eyes, which looked at him beseechingly. He did not know it; but he had entirely bidden adieu to common-sense where Alexia Boucheafen was concerned. He said gently:

"What's the matter? Tell me? Am I to read this?"

"If you will." She let him take the letter; and he saw that it was written in a boyish, wavering hand, and that it commenced affectionately with her name. It was short, for the signature, to which his eyes turned instinctively, was upon the same page, and was, "Your brother, Gustave Boucheafen."

The Doctor repeated it aloud.

"Your brother, Mademoiselle?"

"You have heard me speak of my brother, sir?"

"Certainly—yes! But I thought he was in Paris."

"I thought so too. He was there three months ago, when I last heard from him. But the post he held was poor, miserable, he hated it; and he was threatening then to leave it and come to England, as I had one. He did so a month ago, and has found that the bad could be worse, for he writes that he is penniless, sir, and starving."

"And he writes to you for help, poor child!" exclaimed the Doctor pityingly.

"Yes. But, ah, sir, he is so young—a boy! He is two years younger than I am—only nineteen," Alexia urged deprecatingly. "And whom should he ask, poor Gustave? We have no other kin who care for us."

"Where is your brother?" inquired the Doctor.

"Close here, in London; but I forget the address." She pointed to the letter, which he still held. "Sir, if you read you will understand better far than I can explain."

Doctor Brudenell read the letter—just such a letter as a foolish, impulsive, reckless boy might write, and certainly describing a condition that was desperate enough. The Doctor returned it, and asked doubtfully:

"Mademoiselle, what do you wish me to do? You wish to help him?"

"Ah, sir—yes!" she cried eagerly, and then stopped, faltering. "But I have no money," she said, her head drooping.

The Doctor walked to the end of the room, came back, and stood beside her.

"My poor child, I understand you; but it must not be. Why should the little you earn go to your brother? At the best it would help him only for a very little time, for I see that he says he has no present prospect of employment. In a week or two he would be in his present state again. Something else must be done."

"Ah, sir, it is easy—so easy to speak!" said the governess bitterly. "What else can be done? Who is there that will help him, poor Gustave? He is even poorer, more helpless than I, for in all this England he has not even one friend."

It needed only these words and the glance that accompanied them to turn the doubtful notion that was in the Doctor's mind into a resolve. But he had a sufficient sense of his own imprudence even now to hesitate a little before speaking again.

"Mademoiselle," he said gently, "I know that a lad such as your brother must be often placed at a great disadvantage in his endeavors to get on if, as you say, he is alone and friendless. Being a foreigner increases the difficulty, no doubt. You must let me see if I cannot remedy it."

"You will help him!" cried Alexia eagerly. She rose, her face flushing, her eyes sparkling. It was the first time he had seen them shine so, the first time that a crimson flush had dispelled that curious ivory pallor; her beauty dazzled him; he thought her grateful for the help offered to a brother whom she loved. In her heart, with perfect coolness, she was thinking him a fool, and triumphing in the victory which she foresaw that she would win through his folly. It was her first full knowledge of her power over him. "Tell me what I must do?" she exclaimed.

"Write to your brother, and tell him to come here," returned the Doctor. He spoke quickly, refusing to doubt or falter. "I have no doubt I shall be able to help him to a fitting situation before long. Until then he must remain here. You will have at least the satisfaction of knowing that he is safe then. You—you do not object to the suggestion?" he added with sudden humility, afraid that he might have spoken too coolly, too imperatively. With a sudden movement she seized his hand and pressed it.

"Object—I? Ah, sir, how can I, when you are so good, so more than kind?" She stopped, faltering. "My poor Gustave shall thank you—I cannot. For what can I say but, Thank you a hundred times!"

"Tut, tut!" said the Doctor lightly, recovering his self-possession as she released his hand. "You make too much of it—it is nothing. I am only too pleased to be able to serve you. You will write to your brother?"

"At once, sir." She was turning to the door, when a thought occurred to him—a last lingering touch of prudence and caution made him say:

"Mademoiselle, you have not told me. How did your brother know where you were— where to write to you?"

"By the papers, sir—by what you call the reports of police," she said, turning and replying without the least hesitation. "It was the first thing that he saw, my poor boy, that account of me. But he would not come here or let me know he was in England, lest I should be troubled about him, and he did not wish me to know, besides, that he was poor and distressed. I am sure of that, although he does not tell me."

She left the room, and ran fleetly up-stairs to her own sitting-room. The children were in bed, and there was no one to see her as she drew her writing-case toward her, and wrote swiftly:

"I have succeeded; my cause was won before I had time to plead it. You are at liberty to come here. If, once here, you will succeed in doing what you desire, I cannot tell. It is your affair, not mine. I have done my part. Come then, and remember yours—my brother."

Doctor Brudenell, paying his visit to the governess's sitting-room the next evening to bid his nephews and niece good-night, found there, not the children, but a stranger. His momentary look of surprise vanished as he recollected; and, while he spoke a few rather embarrassed words of greeting and welcome, he keenly scanned Gustave Boucheafen.

He was a handsome young fellow, tall, slender, and dark, and looking very boyish, in spite of some deep lines on the white forehead and about the small, tightly-compressed lips. His clothes were shabby, almost threadbare; there was an air of carelessness, even recklessness, about him, and yet there was something that was far more easy to feel than to describe which proclaimed him to be a gentlemen. All this the Doctor noted as he took the soft slim hand, and answered as briefly as he could the voluble speech of thanks which the young man tendered him, speaking in English less correct than Alexia's and with a certain extravagance of expression and manner which discomfited George Brudenell, and which he decided was wholly French.

But, although embarrassed, as he always was by anything fresh and new, he spoke very kindly and encouragingly to the brother, conscious always of the sister's beautiful eyes resting gently upon him; and, after a few questions asked and answered, he left the two to themselves, and was called out shortly afterward to attend a very stout old gentleman whom he had warned six months before to take his choice between present port-wine and future apoplexy. The old gentleman, being as obstinate as old people of both sexes occasionally are, had heroically chosen the port; and now, according to the account of a flushed messenger, he was enduring the punishment prophesied, and was purple already. The weary Doctor took up his hat resignedly and went out. Alexia Boucheafen, standing idly leaning against the window-frame, negligently listening to what her companion was saying, saw her employer hurrying down the steps and along the hot pavement, upon which the sun had been shining fiercely all day.

"He has gone out," she said, looking round, with a curious inflection in her voice, as though that fact had a bearing upon the conversation that had gone before.

"Already?" cried the young man eagerly. "Better than I hoped. And does he leave his study, laboratory—what does he call it?—unlocked?"

"Yes."

"You are sure?"

"Am I likely to be mistaken?"

"Of course not—no!" He moved across to the door. "Well, come, show me! Come!"

"You are in a hurry," said the governess, not stirring.

"What would you have me do?" he demanded impatiently. "Can we let time and opportunity slip together, with what we have to do?"

"Have we not done enough for the present?" she asked slowly. Calm and cold as she was, a slight irrepressible shudder shook her frame, and he eyed her incredulously.

"Your note used to be different," he said, with a meaning glance. "Enough? What do you mean?"

"I saw it." She looked at him steadily, with unflinching eyes. "I saw him!"

"You did?"

"I did."

"You! What possessed you?"

"I hardly know. I could not help it. I had a fancy that I must."

"You with fancies, you with whims and caprices!" He laughed a laugh of fierce mockery, strode across the room, took her slender wrist in his hand and felt the pulse. "Ah, you are ill, your nerves are out of order, or"—in a different tone—"you suffer from a lapse of memory, perhaps!"

"What do you mean?"—wrestling herself free, and drawing her level brows together in a sudden threatening frown.

He went on as though he had not heard her:

"I hoped that your one relapse would be your last, and pleaded for you, thinking so. It was no easy matter to win you—even you—absolution."

"Bah!" she retorted scoffingly. "Think you I do not know why it was granted? I am valuable, am I not?"

"You were."

"Were!" she cried. "Am I less now because, looking at that dead boy, I for once remembered that I was a woman? You doubt me! Who are you to dare do it? What have you done for the Cause that will weigh in the scales against what I have done? Show me the paltry pin-prick of suffering that you place against my agony?"

"Hush!" he said, in a low tone, and glancing round warningly, evidently taken aback by her sudden vehemence. "You mistake me. I wished merely to remind you."

"Goad me, rather!" she retorted with unabated passion. "I forget! I forget either the blood of the dead or the tortures of the living! I forget the oath I swore with this in my hand!"

Her fingers had been restlessly plucking at the bosom of her gown, and now she held out upon her open hand the tiny roll of red-marked paper. She looked at it for a few moments with dilating eyes, while the color died out of her face and left it impassive marble again. Then she slowly restored the little roll to her breast and turned to the door.

"Come," she said. "I will show you."

CHAPTER VI.

Doctor Brudenell realized very often the fact that the life of a London medical man, however large his practice and solvent his patients, is not by any means an enviable one. Once upon a time, when a red lamp had been a novelty, and the power to write "M. D." after his ordinary signature a delicious dignity, a patient had been to him a prodigy, something precious for its rarity, even if it called him away from his dinner or ruthlessly rang him up in the middle of the night. But that was a long time ago, in the days of his impecunious youth; and now, in his prosperous middle-age, he would often have willingly bartered a good many patients for a little more leisure.

This was particularly the case upon a hot, oppressive night a week later, a night such as London generally experiences in August. It was Saturday, and certainly it was not pleasant, after a week of fatiguing work, to be summoned as soon as he had got into his bedroom, at considerably past eleven o'clock at night, to attend a patient who resided somewhere in the wilds of Holloway.

However, there was no help for it; and the Doctor, philosophically resigning himself, and taking care to be sure that his latch-key was in his pocket, spoke a word to Mrs. Jessop, as a precaution against that worthy woman's putting up the chain of the hall door before she went to bed, and let himself out. It was a fine night, hot as it was, with a large bright moon hardly beginning to wane, and myriads of stars. Doctor Brudenell, as good and quick a walker now as he had been twenty years before, thought lightly of the distance between his own house and that of his patient, and soon reached his destination. It was little that he could do—in fact, he had been sent for without real need—and it was not much after twelve o'clock when he reached the railway-arch which spans the Holloway Road. He stopped for a moment, and looked up, thinking what a black bar it seemed in the yellow moonlight, and how oddly quiet the streets were, which all day long were teeming with noisy life. Most of the shops were closed, and only a few straggling foot-passengers were to be seen. Only for a moment did he thus glance about him, taking his hat off to push the damp hair from his forehead, for his quick walk had made him warm. Then he walked on under the arch, to stop before it was half traversed, for a hand suddenly placed upon his shoulders brought him to a halt.

"Your pardon, sir," said a voice in his ear. "You are a doctor, I believe?"

"I am!" The Doctor tried in the gloom of the arch to make out the face of the inquirer, but in vain. He could only tell that it was a young man by his voice and gestures, and he saw that he was considerably taller than himself.

"Doctor Brudenell, I think?"

"I am Doctor Brudenell. What is wanted?"

"Yourself, sir, if you please. A person—my—brother—is ill—almost dying, it is feared. Will you accompany me to him? There is no time to be lost."

"What is the matter with him?" asked the Doctor.

"Sir, you will know when you see him. I"—with a deprecatory shrug of the shoulders—"can I tell?"

"But is it a fit, a fever, an accident? What is it?" asked Doctor Brudenell impatiently. "You must know that."

"Sir, it cannot be a fever, since an hour ago he was well. Pray, sir, will you come? He is very ill. Delay is dangerous."

The man moved on as he spoke, and the Doctor moved with him, for his arm was still clasped by the stranger's strong supple fingers. But outside the archway he stopped.

"Stay! Why do you come to me? Have you no regular medical attendant?"

"We have not, sir. As to why I come to you—I have heard of you, that is all. I reached your house almost as you left it, and have followed you, and waited. Pray come, sir, I entreat you. There is a carriage waiting here."

A carriage was standing just outside the arch—an ordinary-looking close carriage, drawn by a light-colored horse, and driven by a coachman who was singularly muffled up, considering the heat of the night. The Doctor mechanically noticed that there were no lamps to the carriage, as, in obedience to the eager pressure of his companion's hand, he got in. The other followed, shutting the door smartly behind him, and the vehicle started instantly.

Doctor Brudenell, leaning back in his corner, looked curiously—as well as the dimness of the carriage would let him—with the keen eyes of a man accustomed to weigh and observe, at his companion, who, with his hands in his pockets and his hat pulled down over his brows, appeared to be half asleep. He was a very handsome man, that was certain—face dark and clear cut, complexion swarthy, figure at once lithe and muscular, and some years under thirty. There was a turn of the throat, a trick of movement, when he presently changed his position restlessly, that perplexed the watcher. The Doctor fancied that he must have seen this man before, but he could not remember where.

"Is it far?" he asked suddenly. It must be, he thought. They had been in the carriage at least a quarter of an hour; the horse had been going at a swift trot, and now there was no sign of slackening speed.

The young man started, and opened his eyes.

"It is not now, sir. We shall soon be there—in time, I hope."

He stamped twice upon the floor of the carriage impatiently, as though in anxiety; but the sound seemed to act as a signal, for the driver instantly whipped up the horse, and the speed was increased—almost doubled. The curtains of the windows were down, and the Doctor drew one of them aside and peered out. They were in a street he did not know, badly paved, badly lighted, squalid, flanked by rows of high mean houses, half of which seemed empty, for hardly a light shone from their windows. He looked round.

"Where are we?"

"We are close there, sir."

"But what street is this? I don't know it in the least."

"Sir, I do not know it; but I know that in a moment we shall be there."

The Doctor sank back into his corner again resignedly. He was fatigued, sleepy, put out. Just then he most heartily wished that this young man had found some one else to attend to the wants of his brother. He must be crazy—to have gone all that distance after a doctor, and then to follow and accost one in the street! It was as queer a thing in its way as his twenty years in the profession had brought to his knowledge. Thinking over this his eyelids drooped; he no longer saw the dim figure of his companion and was startled when presently the carriage stopped with a jerk. In a moment the young man had opened the door, sprung out, and was saying:

"We are here. Alight, sir, if you please."

Doctor Brudenell, confused and sleepy still, did so, looking about him. He was in a narrow paved court, entirely unlighted, closed in at the lower end by what seemed to be a huge deserted stack of warehouses and fenced upon the farther side by the blank walls and regular rows of narrow windows of what had evidently been a manufactory; but the windows were broken; a door hung swinging upon its hinges; it was evident that this place was unused and deserted too. Upon the side where he stood were a couple of old houses, bare and desolate, with broken windows, broken railings—dark, silent—the most dismal houses the Doctor had ever seen.

At the door of the first of these, where a faint light was visible in one of the lower windows as the carriage stopped, the young man tapped cautiously with his hand three times. In another moment the door was softly opened, the figure of the opener being lost in the gloom within. On the broken door-step the Doctor hesitated; he was not a timid man, but this all seemed very strange. However, he obeyed the pressure of the hand laid upon his arm, and entered; glancing behind him as he did so, he saw that the carriage had disappeared.

The door was gently closed; and he stood in absolute darkness, hesitating, wondering. He fancied he heard cautious feet stealing across the bare floor of the hall; but not another sound broke the oppressive brooding silence of the close, musty-smelling old house. In another moment he would have spoken, have demanded the meaning of all this, when a faint gleam of light appeared at the end of the hall, and from the lower stairs a man's hand and arm became visible, holding a lamp. A hand was laid upon his arm at the same moment, and the voice of his summoner spoke quietly in his ear:

"Your patient is ready, sir. Come, if you please."

The speaker went toward the stairs, and the light was withdrawn. The Doctor followed him for a few paces, then stopped abruptly.

"Down-stairs!" he said incredulously.

"Sir, he was too bad to be moved."

"I see. Go before, if you please."

The light glimmered faintly at the foot of the staircase again, and the Doctor followed his conductor down, noting that the steps were dirty and bare, that the stone passage-way at the bottom was also dirty and bare, that, for all the indications that there were to the contrary, this was an absolutely unfurnished house. As he reached the last stair he looked keenly at the man who held the lamp—a middle-aged man, loose-jointed and loosely dressed, with iron-gray hair and a scar upon his cheek. He spoke with a slightly foreign accent, and, with a bow, moved aside from the doorway in which he stood.

"You are welcome, sir; I thank you. Enter, if you please."

Doctor Brudenell did so, then started and stopped involuntarily. A sick man, a man on the point of dying—were they mad enough to keep him in a room such as this? A room? A sty, rather! The door was stone, with a few sacks spread upon it; the windows were secured by crazy shutters, the only table was formed by boards laid upon two old barrels, and the two or three chairs were broken. The only other piece of furniture or semblance of furniture was an old couch, the horse-hair covering tattered, straggling pieces of the stuffing hanging down. Lying upon it was the figure of a man, with some roughly-applied bandages about his head and face.

Strange as it all was, the sight of this man, the cause of his being there, restored to the Doctor his professional coolness and self-possession. He was a medical man—this was his patient. He advanced, and with rapid deft fingers removed the bandages, laying bare a face so horribly disfigured that, practiced as he was, he felt his own turn pale. He spoke quickly and aloud, knowing that the sick man was insensible, and looking at the other two.

"What's this? What has happened to this man? He is burnt!"

"As you say, sir." The gray-haired man, still holding the lamp, bowed.

"Most horribly burnt—and with chemicals. Is it not so?"

"It is, sir."

"There has been an explosion. He was trying to do something with them—probably combine them—he made a mistake in his method or calculations, and they exploded," said the Doctor rapidly.

"Again you are right, sir." The two men exchanged swift glances of mingled admiration and contempt—admiration of the Doctor's quickness and lucidity, contempt of him for being there. He did not see them; he was continuing his examination of the insensible man. The injuries to the head and face were the worst, but the throat, chest, and arms were also burned severely. Doctor Brudenell rose from the knee upon which he had sunk down to pursue his examination.

"You should have told me what the case was," he said sternly, looking at the young man. "You bring me here in ignorance, and I am absolutely helpless. I have no materials for treating injuries such as these. I require lint, oil, bandages."

"They are here," said the gray-haired man quietly; and as his companion, in obedience to a motion of his hand, left the room, he looked at the Doctor, and asked anxiously, "Sir, can you save his life?"

"I don't know—it depends upon his constitution—of which I know nothing—and the care that is bestowed upon him. But"—with a glance round the wretched apartment— "he will not live if he stays here."

"He will not stay here."

The Doctor said no more, for the young man came back with bandages, lint, and oil. All three had evidently been purchased in anticipation of their being wanted. The Doctor applied them as well as he could, by the dim light of the lamp. The patient moved and moaned, but he did not open his eyes or show any signs of consciousness; the other two did not speak once. His task concluded, the Doctor turned to them abruptly.

"He had better be moved at once; he cannot pass the night here—indeed, he should have been got up-stairs at the first. If there is any assistance that you can call it will be as well. He is utterly helpless. He must be carried."

"Good!" said the elder man quietly, and with the suspicion of a mocking smile at the corners of his mouth. "Explain, sir, if you please. Carried where?"

"Up-stairs, of course!"

"Up-stairs!" Both men laughed, but only the elder echoed the word. "Impossible, sir!" he said coolly.

"But I tell you he must be moved!" exclaimed the Doctor impatiently. "You have risked his life already by your delay."

"Reassure yourself, sir," said the other, in the same tone as before. "He shall be moved—I have said it!"

"Then where, if not up-stairs?"

"Out of the house."

"Out of the house—in this condition? You must be out of your mind! It will kill him!"

Doctor Brudenell was excited. He rebelled against this treatment of his patient—as his patient. As merely a man he would not have cared.

"Kill him—so be it!"

The speaker shrugged his shoulders, with a smile that expanded the scar on his cheek, and the Doctor involuntarily moderated his tone. He instinctively recognized that he had spoken too bluntly, too hastily to this man, who looked impenetrable.

"You must really understand," he urged, "the great risk of what you are about to do. This man's condition is dangerous now; the shock to the system may be so great that even with the best of care he will not recover. By doing what you propose you seriously jeopardize what chance he has of life. When do you intend to move him?"

"Sir, at once!"

"What—now—in the middle of the night?"

"Exactly, sir."

"Preposterous!" the Doctor cried excitedly. "It shall not be done!"

"Indeed. And who, sir, will prevent it?"

"If necessary, I will."

The man put down the lamp upon the boards that served as a table, put his hands to his sides, and laughed. Not loudly or heartily, but with intense mocking enjoyment, as at something too grotesquely absurd for speech. Then suddenly, exerting a surprising amount of strength for so old a man, he put his two hands upon the shoulders of the slightly-built Doctor, and, holding him so, stood looking down at him tauntingly, laughing still.

"You will—you will prevent! Monsieur the Doctor, you are a hero. You are alone, you don't know where, with you don't know whom; it is one o'clock in the morning, no one in your household knows where to find you, and yet you will prevent! You stand in a house where your body might remain undiscovered for years; but still you defy, you threaten! By Heaven, my noble physician, you are brave!"

He loosened his hold and leaned against the improvised table, laughing still in the same suppressed manner, and glancing at the young man, who replied to this dreadful mirth with a sarcastic smile.

George Brudenell, almost staggering as the strong hands released him, was stupefied for the moment. He was no coward, but he suddenly realized the utter helplessness of his position. Where was he? He did not know. Who were these men, who met alone in this deserted house at midnight? He did not know. He was a weaker man than either; and how many more of them might there not be hidden within hearing distance now? If they chose to do him violence—to murder him, in short—he would be totally incapable of offering any adequate resistance. He was trapped, and he felt it; for the moment the knowledge appalled him, but he strove to regain both his wits an courage.

"You have the advantage, sir," he said, addressing the elder man; "and you use your superiority of numbers well. As for this man, you take the responsibility if you move him. It is none of mine! I have done what I can, and all I can. Show me to the door."

"A moment, sir, if you please!" The younger man looked at the elder with a glance of remonstrance, as though he thought his companion in his last speech and action had gone too far. "You are forgetting an important item, sir—your fee."

"I want no fee, and will take none! Show me to the door, I say!"

He turned toward the doorway. By himself he would have stumbled up the stairs down which he had been enticed; but the elder man seized him by the shoulder. He spoke now in a tone almost as courteous as that which he had just used had been insulting.

"Your pardon! A moment, sir, if you please. You were called here——"

"Trapped here!" interposed the Doctor angrily.

"Well, well"—the other spoke blandly, soothingly, as though to a restive child—"trapped here, if you will. A word—what does it matter? Permit me to finish. There are two things to do, sir, and you have done but one."

"I will do nothing more!"

George Brudenell was thoroughly master of himself again now, and he flung off the hand upon his shoulder. The young man moved and stood between him and the door, and the elder resumed coolly:

"A difficult thing, since it has something like death to answer for"—with a glance at the senseless disfigured form upon the couch; "but an easy thing—a mere bagatelle to a man such as you—a skillful chemist, a practiced handler of chemicals. Monsieur, you will do what yonder bungler failed to do—you will, if you please, combine these chemicals."

"I will not!" The Doctor's temper was roused; the thought that he had been so tricked made him forget the danger he was in. He spoke without any signs of fear now, and faced the pair. Comprehension he had not, but suspicion he had, and he spoke it out hardily. "I will not!" he repeated. "Whatever villainy it is that you perpetrate here, I will have no hand in it. To whatever atrocious use it is that you design to put the things you speak of, I say that I am glad that they have turned upon one scoundrel at least. It is useless to put these chemicals before me—I swear that I will not touch them! I would sooner cut off my right hand!"

"*Ma foi*, monsieur"—again the elder man smiled!—"you are likely, if you remain obstinate, to lose more than that! Come—consider, sir,—reflect. You are helpless, and we are impatient; your summer nights are short, and we have much to do. Come, then—speak!"

"Ah," cried the younger man suddenly, but in the suppressed tones which both seemed to use habitually—"Hush!"

Doctor Brudenell had heard nothing—could hear nothing, although he listened eagerly; but it seemed that the sound, whatever it might have been, had alarmed the two men. It was evidently repeated, for the lamp was put out instantly, and he felt himself forcibly thrust into what seemed to be a cupboard and heard the key turned in the lock.

For a few moments George Brudenell was dazed again—stupefied. He was so utterly amazed that he could hardly believe that it was not all a dream. Was this the latter half of the nineteenth century....was he in the heart of London? Then suddenly he realized his position, tried to suppress his very breathing and the beating of his heart, for there was a sound of footsteps upon the creaking stairs, some one else entered the room, there was the scratching of a match, and a pale thread of light crept under the door of his prison, showing that the lamp had been relighted. He listened intently, jealously, straining every nerve to hear and to understand. Voices whispered; he could distinguish the tones of the two men, but not their words, the muffled muttering was too low; then there came a cry, followed by a rapid movement toward the door which shut him from these strange whisperers—more, a hand was even laid upon the lock and the key was partly turned. Then there came a scuffle, almost a struggle, a sound of something being dragged along the bare boards, and the voice of the elder man muttering fiercely, threateningly. The Doctor, as the footsteps retreated and the savage, repressed sounds died away into a distant murmur, leaned against the damp wall of his prison, and fought with a fresh perplexity. The new-comer into that gloomy house of wickedness and mystery was a woman! He had heard the sweep of heavy skirts as his door was approached, and that one shrill, hardly-stifled cry had surely been in a woman's voice! Then the pale thread of light was withdrawn, the sound of footsteps moved toward the door, and a horrible fear assailed him. Was he to be left there to break his way out into light or to die in darkness? The notion was horrible; his self-control failed him; and with his clenched hands he hammered upon the panels of the door, calling out loudly that he would not be left there, trapped like a rat, and appealing to them to let him out.

There was a pause, more hurried, unintelligible whispering, then footsteps drew near the door, and outside a voice spoke—the elder man's.

"Be silent, and no harm will be done you. Be patient, sir, and you shall be released."

"When?" demanded Doctor Brudenell.

"When we have done what we have to do. Until then, silence!"

Again the footsteps and the light withdrew, and the Doctor was left in absolute silence and complete darkness, to fight as well as he could with his sense of utter helplessness and the violent beating of his heart. The struggle lasted only for a short time as he found out afterward, but in the passing it seemed an age. Then the pale gleam of light crept again beneath the door, and there came the sound of footsteps; the two men had returned. He could hear that they were raising a heavy body with painful difficulty, for there were low moans and one deep groan—they were moving the almost dying man.

Another and longer interval of profound darkness, of brooding silence followed, until the footsteps again returned, the door was thrown open, and he stepped out, dazed by the light, feeble as it was. The lamp was held by the man with the scar on his cheek, the couch upon which the wounded man had lain was empty; a faint trace of light shone through the chinks of the crazy shutters—it was almost morning.

"You are free, sir," said his captor calmly and in a tone of perfect indifference, cutting short the useless words of wrath and indignation which fell from the Doctor's lips. "Go, and hasten, if you please; the night is nearly over! The carriage in which you came waits."

"I shall not use it; I will go alone, and on foot." He stepped toward the door, anxious just then for nothing except to get free of the detested house, but, as before, the man's hand was brought down upon his shoulder.

"Your pardon, sir—you will go as you came, and with the same companion. You need not fear—no harm of any kind will be done you. I have pledged my word that you shall depart as you came, and I will keep it. Good! Depart then, if you please."

Realizing the utter futility of lingering or speaking, Doctor Brudenell was prudent. He obeyed without remonstrance or delay. He mounted the stairs, crossed the bare hall, and left the house. In a moment his arm was seized by the younger man, he was hustled into the carriage which had brought him, and driven off at a pace so swift that he had the sense at once to abandon the design of leaping out which he had hastily formed. But that would have been impossible had the vehicle moved slowly, for the eyes of his companion were keenly on the alert, as he could not fail to see. Not a word upon either side had been spoken when, some half an hour later, the carriage suddenly stopped, he was thrust out as strongly and roughly as he had been hustled in; and, as he stood, dazed by the events of this extraordinary night and the rush of fresh sweet air, the coachman drove rapidly away.

George Brudenell looked about him like one bereft of reason. He had no idea of the route by which he had been driven, and it was only after looking for some time at the houses about him that he discovered where he was, for he felt as perplexed and confused as though he had been voyaging through the air in a balloon. Slowly he recognized his surroundings—he was close upon the confines of Victoria Park. Not a sound broke the silence, not a form was visible, the dawn was brightening rosily in the east. He drew out his watch; it was just three o'clock on Sunday morning.

CHAPTER VII.

It was not to be wondered at that Doctor Brudenell, coming down to breakfast at the usual time some five hours later, should have looked what Mrs. Jessop called "as pale as the very table-cloth itself," or that he should have but little desire either for the meal or his Sunday paper. The very children, coming in by and by to bid him good-morning before going to church, loudly expressed their astonishment in a shrill trio as to Uncle George's funny looks, and rather rebelled at the unusually curt greeting and dismissal which he gave them. Even the governess's eyes opened a little wider as she looked at him, but she gave him her hand with her usual shadowy smile, and expressed no interest or surprise. Not that she would have learned anything had she been as concerned as she was indifferent, for George Brudenell, reflecting upon and recalling his adventure of the night before, fully realizing his own position, had come to the conclusion to dismiss and forget it if he could, and to speak of it to no one.

The Doctor was a shrewd man, and, understanding his fellow-men in their mental as well as their physical natures, knew very well that such a story, if it were not entirely discredited, would be at any rate doubted and caviled at. The general opinion would be that there was some truth in it, but not much. He was a sensitive man, disliking and dreading ridicule, and he came to the conclusion that no possible good could result from his publishing the story. He did not know the men—the street, the house, and the locality were alike unknown to him. When speech could do no good, could throw no light, silence became wise. He would be silent.

He fell asleep in his comfortable chair presently, and waking up in a couple of hours, was cheerful—more cheerful than usual. It happened that he was not called out, and that there were no visits that he was absolutely obliged to make, and so he spent the day about the house and garden, enjoying his leisure almost boyishly. He romped with the children in the garden, swung them, played ball with them, would have even run races with them perhaps, as they earnestly besought him to do, had the weather been cooler. Suddenly he caught sight of the perfect face of Alexia Boucheafen at a window, with her brother beside her, and, meeting her dark eyes, was a little abashed for the moment. He did not play with the children any more, and the young rebels wondered why, after being in such an absolutely seraphic temper, he should turn cross so suddenly. Perhaps it was not her watching that vexed him, but the scrutiny of that other pair of eyes. For, slowly and reluctantly, George Brudenell had by this time made up his mind that, with every desire to like this handsome young Gustave Boucheafen, he could not do so.

"Prejudice, no doubt," said the Doctor to himself, when presently, after having discreetly quieted his nephews and niece by a gift of sixpence each, he sat down to smoke a cigar in his study; "but upon my word I shall be glad when the young fellow is out of the house. Well, this post at Langley's will be a pretty good chance for him if he chooses to stick to it. If he has any sense he will. I'll tell her this evening, by the way."

He did not see Alexia again until the children were sleeping and the twilight was fading at the approach of night. Then, looking from his study window, he saw her, tall and erect, in her black dress, pacing the gravel walk beside the trimly-kept lawn. Her brother was at her side again, and they were talking earnestly, absorbedly—he with his usual redundancy of gesture, she with unfailing calmness. It seemed that they were arguing about something—he urging, she resisting—for presently she flung off the hand which he had placed upon her arm, and turned her back upon him. His face darkened, the lines about his mouth grew hard, he spoke a word or two, regarding her with a curious smile; and then, turning upon his heel, without waiting for a reply, went into the house. Doctor Brudenell paused, stood hesitating for a few moments, then went out and joined her.

She would have moved away as he approached her, but, with his usual diffident, shy manner toward her, he begged her to remain for a little while, as he had something to say. Then she turned and walked beside him—her eyes fixed intently upon him in the gray dusk. Had he kept his eyes upon her face, instead of nervously looking away, he would have seen upon it curiosity, and signs of apprehension too scornful and contemptuous for fear.

"I will only keep you a moment, Mademoiselle. I wanted to say, that with regard to your brother——"

"Yes, sir."

"I am glad to tell you that I have been successful in my efforts on his behalf. There is, in the business-house of a friend of mine, a post vacant which I think will probably suit him, and which he is likely to fill creditably. Indeed, I may say that it only awaits his acceptance to-morrow."

Her eyes had wandered away from his face when he began to speak; now they came back quickly, gleaming brightly in the dusk. He was taken aback, and yet he wondered why, for she merely repeated:

"To-morrow?"

"I was merely going to add that to-morrow an interview will probably settle the business."

"Ah, sir—you see you are so kind, so good! How can I thank you—what can I say?"

George Brudenell, listening, looking, lost his head. He had meant to tell her what he had to tell quietly and coolly, make light of the thanks which only embarrassed him, and so go back soberly to his book and cigar again. But he met her eyes, heard her voice, and the resolve was gone. He never knew what it was that he said to Alexia Boucheafen—in what words he clothed his passion, in what phrases he pleaded. He only knew that she listened for a moment impassively, that the next time the cold blankness of her face was gone, that it was replaced by a look of scorn, incredulity, pity, contempt—he did not know what—that an instant later she had wrenched away the hand he had taken, had burst into a laugh that rang out shrilly in the gloom, and that he was standing alone, bewildered, thinking that her laugh had sounded like an echo of the laugh that he had heard last night in that mysterious house—the laugh of the gray-haired man with the scar upon his cheek.

Alexia Boucheafen, moving with a rapidity unlike her usual slow graceful motion, had rushed into the house and up to her sitting-room. Her brother was there, evidently waiting for her, but he was not waiting for anything like this. She looked at him for a moment, then drew herself into a chair, and shrieked with hysterical laughter. Gustave Boucheafen was cautious. He hurried to the door, shut and locked it, returned and grasped her arm firmly.

"What is this? Control yourself—consider!"

Her wild laughter was already dying away; it was evident that she had to exercise rigid self-control to prevent it from turning to still wilder sobbing. She sat for a few moments with her hands pressed over her eyes, her breast heaving convulsively. When she looked at him, rising as she did so, her eyes dilated and gleamed.

"This night," she said—"this night of all others to choose!"

"To choose for what?"

"To make love to me! Think of it!"

"Bah! What did I tell you but just now?" he returned sullenly, releasing her arm. "You laughed. Fool as he was—tool as you had made him, he was not fool enough for that, you said. Eh—was he not? I knew how it would be. Did I not tell you so before I even entered this house?" Looking at her, he laughed grimly. "What a fool—an idiot!"

"Bah!" she retorted, with a bitter smile. "What, think you, does he know? I could laugh at myself, for I am almost sorry!"

"For him?"

"Why not? He is a good man in his way, and he has been kind. Don't look at me like that!" she cried with sudden passion, a swift rush of blood tinting the pallor of her cheeks. "What do you think he is to me, this man, but the tool I have made him? He has not harmed me—he represents nothing that has harmed me; and I would not hurt him, as I would not hurt a child."

"Ah, that is all?" He looked at her keenly. "Good—and yet last night——"

"Well," she said defiantly, "last night I saved him. What then? He could do us no harm—he had done us good, and our use for him was nearly over—I may say now that it is over."

"Unless we fail."

"Fail!" she echoed contemptuously.

"What did you say to him?" he asked after a moment's pause.

"Nothing. What should I say? I rushed away. What does it matter? I shall not see him again."

"True." He glanced at the clock. "Eight," he said, turning toward the door, as though to close the conversation by leaving the room. "You will not forget the time?"

"I shall not."

"And," he added warningly, "you will not blench—this time?"

She did not hear him. She had drawn from her breast the tiny roll of red-marked paper; and, holding it upon the palm of her hand, was looking at it with a curiously intent and bitter smile.

"Good!" said Gustave Boucheafen, with satisfaction; and he went out and left her.

CHAPTER VIII., AND LAST.

George Brudenell, having passed a restless and troubled evening, passed also a restless and dream-haunted night, coming down to breakfast the next morning jaded and out of sorts. He could not for a moment dismiss from his memory that interview in the garden last night, or explain to himself the meaning of Alexia Boucheafen's extraordinary conduct. What was he to understand from it? Had her behavior been prompted by astonishment, indecision, or annoyance? He did not know; and he could make nothing of it. The Doctor ate no breakfast; but came to the conclusion that he must see her again, and that as soon as possible; his earnestness and anxiety conquered his diffidence. He rang the bell for Mrs. Jessop, and asked if Mademoiselle were down-stairs yet? He wished to see her.

Mrs. Jessop, looking curiously at her master, went and returned. No, Mademoiselle was not down yet; she had complained last night of headache. Was it anything very particular; and should she be called? Not on any account. The Doctor picked up the paper that he had forgotten to read, and went to his consulting-room.

It was empty, for it was not yet his usual hour for receiving patients. To fill up the time and to escape from his own thoughts he opened the paper. The first thing that caught his eye and changed his indifference to involuntarily interest was the announcement, in the most sensational terms, of two supposed dynamite outrages which had taken place on the previous night, resulting in the partial wreck of one house and the almost total destruction of another, together with the death of the Russian police-agent who lived in it.

It was just at this time that some such paragraph formed the chief sensational "tit-bit" of almost every newspaper, and outraged public opinion was ready to run wild upon the subject. The Doctor, excited, horrified, interested, read the account. The two explosions had taken place almost simultaneously, and had evidently been caused by the same kind of infernal machine, whether containing dynamite or some other explosive was not quite certain. As for the police-agent who had been killed, it was known that he had been threatened by some secret society, supposed to have lurking-places in various parts of London, he having a year or two before been mainly instrumental in the breaking up of a Nihilist society in Russia, and in bringing to the scaffold its chief and most active member, a young Russian of noble birth. The second explosion, which had done less damage, and was happily unattended by any serious results beyond the partial wrecking of the house, was at the private residence of a well-known English Detective. The latest news was that there was a clue to the perpetrators of both outrages.

Doctor Brudenell tossed aside the paper, shrugging his shoulders as at a madman's irresponsible rashness and folly, and turned his attention to the patient who just then came in. That patient and the many succeeding patients thought the Doctor odd this morning, brusque, absent, constrained, gruff. He was thinking of Alexia, wondering what she would say to him, wondering still more what he would say to her. The room was empty at last; and he went back to the dining-room and rang again for Mrs. Jessop. He could not face the day's round of work without seeing her first. Mrs. Jessop was asked to inquire if Mademoiselle could see him now. The housekeeper went, and returned looking rather puzzled. Mademoiselle was not down-stairs yet, although her breakfast was cold and the children were waiting to begin their lessons. Mrs. Jessop was alarmed; her master wondered, and felt anxious.

"She may be ill," he said; "you say she complained last night. Go and see. Stay—I'll come up-stairs with you!"

He did so. At the governess's door Mrs. Jessop knocked softly and waited, knocked loudly and waited. Then, in obedience to a gesture from the Doctor, she tried to open the door. The handle yielded instantly; and she, looking in, cried out:

"Sir, she isn't here!"

The bed was untouched, had not been slept in. The housekeeper looked frightened at the Doctor's white face as he glanced round the room.

"Call her brother. He has not been seen either. Quick!"

A couple of curious maids, lingering on the stairs, ran up the next flight to obey. There was the sound of knocking at panels, a pause, and a cry at which George Brudenell felt his heart turn cold, for he understood what it meant. That room was vacant too!

He sent all the women away, and examined Alexia's apartment himself. There was not a line of writing, not a trace or clue of any sort to explain this mystery. A few articles of clothing were scattered carelessly about on the chairs and on the sofa; a faded flower which she had worn yesterday in the bosom of her gown lay upon the toilet-table. The poor blossom was dry and withered; he took it up in his hand, crushed it, and flung its powdery fragments from him. Then he came out, shut the door, and went straight down-stairs and out to his waiting carriage.

George Brudenell, afterward looking back upon that day, wondered how he got through it; but he did, and reached home at last, to be met by Mrs. Jessop, who, in the last stage of amazement, indignation, and perplexity, informed him that Mademoiselle and her brother had not yet made their appearance. He had expected that, and, cutting short the good woman's garrulous comments and questions, sent her away. He left his dinner untouched, and went into his consulting-room; and, as he waited for the usual influx of patients, strove to understand, to think. People came in, and he attended to them and watched them go; they told him, some of them, that he looked out of sorts and pale, and he laughed, saying that he was all right. The evening wore away, it grew late, every one in the house had retired but himself. It was nearly twelve o'clock; and he was still sitting, with his head in his hands, trying to solve the problem that perplexed him. Suddenly he started up, and listened. There were footsteps outside— rapid, cautious—a key was placed in the lock, and the door yielded. He darted out into the hall, and grasped the arm of the stealthily-entering figure.

"Alexia!"

With a swift gesture she signed to him to go back into the room, entered after him, and cautiously shut and locked the door. Then with another rapid movement she pulled aside her veil and stood looking at him. He was too astonished to speak, but he saw that she was breathless, intensely pale, that her dress was slightly disordered, and that in the eyes which he knew that he had never understood there was an expression which he could read at last—a look of mingled defiance and fear.

"Sir, will you save me?"

"Save you!" In his bewilderment he could only confusedly echo her words. She moved a pace nearer to him.

"Yes, save me. Last night you said you loved me; but I do not plead to you for that. I plead because I am a woman, alone, friendless, lost without your aid. Sir, will you give it—will you save me?"

"From whom? From what?"

"From the hands of the police, who are now, as I speak, on my track; from the Russian Government, to which I shall be delivered; from the death, or worth than death, which their sleuth-hounds will mete out to me."

"Death! Good heavens, what have you been doing?"

She laughed, glanced round the room, caught up the paper which lay where he had put it down, and pointed to the column which he had read.

"That!" she cried.

"That? What do you mean?"

"I mean that I killed that man," she answered, deliberately. "I placed the infernal machine by his door, and so took the vengeance which I swore to take a year ago, when he took prisoner and gave to torture and death my lover. I failed once, I failed twice; last night I succeeded. He is dead!"

"You murdered this man?

"Yes, as my lover was murdered, as my brother was murdered, as my mother and my sister are being murdered in Siberia, as my father died, murdered in the dungeons of St. Peter and St. Paul. And for what? For daring to act, to speak, to read, to think; for striving to be men and women, for revolting against the horrible tyranny which crushed them as it crushes millions! That was their crime. Bah! what do you know, you English, of brutality, of force, of cruelty, of slavery? You play with the words, and think you have the thing!"

She looked at him as he shrank from her, horrified, unable to grasp or believe her words. Again she laughed bitterly, and, putting her hand into the bosom of her dress, drew out a little roll of paper, and held it toward him. The Doctor drew back. It had suddenly become horrible. He faltered:

"What is it?"

"The last lines of farewell which my lover contrived to have sent to me from his prison the day before they butchered him," she answered, steadily. "He bade me farewell, and called upon me to avenge him. It was redder then than now, for even the blood of an innocent man fades with time; and he wrote this with his blood. With it in my hand, with the memory of his face, when they dragged him away from me forever, always before me, I swore I would obey his last prayer. It is done. His murderer is dead!"

She spoke with an air of dreary triumph, a dreadful exultation that chilled her listener's blood. This was not the woman he had loved, upon whom he had poured out all his long-guarded stores of devotion and passion—this terrible, beautiful, avenging Medusa! His utter confusion and bewilderment were patent to her; as he sank into a chair, she drew a pace nearer to him, speaking rapidly, never pausing except when he himself interrupted her, never halting for a word.

"Sir, listen! I am in your power, since without your aid I cannot escape. I should have been a prisoner now had I not thought of you and had about me the key of your door. I thought you would save me—I think you will, for I have already saved you."

"Me!" he exclaimed, wonderingly.

"You! Think you I do not know where you were taken on Saturday night?"

"You knew! Then——"

"I was there—yes. I knew you would be waylaid and taken there. I knew what you would be asked to do—first, to attend to the injuries of the foolish one among us who had tried to do what he could not do; secondly, to finish what he had begun. You are a braver man than I thought you, and you refused. Without those chemicals we were helpless, for it is those that were used last night. In that deserted house—our meeting-place at intervals for the past year—your dead body might have lain undiscovered for months—would have lain undiscovered in all probability—for you were dealing with desperate men, and you defied them. I went there, as I have done twice before since I lived here, and I pleaded for you and saved you. But I could not have done it except for one thing—I took with me what they wanted. Gustave understands chemicals, and how to combine them; he came here, after I had lied to you about him—for all that story that I told you was one great lie, told because I knew something of my power over you, and that you would probably act as you did—hoping that he could here possess himself of the chemicals that were needed, and which we could not obtain without too great risk of discovery. You believed every word of the story with which I befooled you; he came here, and obtained them easily."

Her audacity, her frankness were almost brutal. His bewilderment was subsiding, but he revolted more and more, understanding so little of the horrible tree of which such a woman as this was the poisoned and poisoning fruit.

"Your brother?" he said, withdrawing from her a little farther. "How did he become possessed of them here?"

"My brother!" she cried, laughing. "He is not my brother; his name is Boucheafen no more than mine. My name! I have almost forgotten what it is, I have borne so many that are false; were I to tell you it you would be no wiser. Where, you ask, did he get the chemicals? From your laboratory. We stole them; look, examine, and you will find them missing!"

She stopped, turning with dilating eyes toward the window, as footsteps approached. They passed, and she turned back again, once more drawing a step nearer to him, fascinating him with the light of her brilliant inflexible eyes.

"Sir, listen again. You have been deceived, as I have shown, but you do not know how much. You recollect the day upon which you saw me first?"

"Yes."

"I told you that I had been robbed; it was a lie. The man that you saw attack me meant to murder me."

"To murder you?"

"Yes. Sir, once more. You don't know what they are, these secret societies, these hidden leagues moulded by Russian oppression and tyranny, these cliques, of which hate, vengeance, extermination, are the watchwords. Knowing so well what treachery is, they are jealous of the faith of their members. Death punishes treachery, and I had been treacherous, and death was my sentence. The Cause avenges itself; the appointed man accepted his appointed task. The man who threatened you that night—that old man, our chief—saved me."

George Brudenell passed his hand over his forehead. The feeling which had assailed him when he was a prisoner in the mysterious house assailed him again—the involuntary doubt as to the reality of what he saw and heard. Still with her relentless eyes fixed upon him, she went on:

"I had been treacherous—I will tell you how. There belonged to us a lad, a boy, almost a child—he was innocent, simple; he was our errand boy, cat's-paw—what you will; and he did what you have done, fell in love with me—because I am beautiful, perhaps. Bah! Many men have loved me—it is nothing. We suspected him, thought him false; with the Cause to suspect is to condemn. He was condemned, and to me was allotted the task of striking him. I meant to do it, I swore to do it. At the last moment my courage failed me—perhaps I pitied him—and I spared him. The sentence passed upon him was passed also upon me."

"And he?"

"He?" She met his look with a gloomy smile. "The Cause does not forgive unless for its own good, as it afterward forgave me. Our chief absolved me, for I was useful—so useful that my one act of treachery, my one moment of weakness, was condoned. For him—what was he? An untrustworthy tool merely. Another hand struck the blow which I had been appointed to strike. He died as I nearly died." She stopped and smiled in the same gloomy way. "No suspicion struck you when his body lay there yonder, and I stood beside you, looking at his dead face!"

"That boy!" cried George Brudenell, horrified.

"That boy," she assented.

There was a pause, during which the Doctor rose and drew back from the tall, splendidly-poised figure, as firm and erect as he had ever seen it. He did not realize yet the blow that had fallen upon him, the blank in his life that would come later; but he felt as though he were struggling in a sea of horror, and was unable to disguise his shrinking from her, his avoidance of her, the woman to whom yesterday he had offered his love humbly, and whom he had besought to be his wife. He asked coldly, not looking at her:

"What can I do?"

"Sir, I have told you—save me. We were seen last night, the clue was followed up, and we were surprised an hour ago in our most secret meeting-place. Three of us were taken—all would have been but for the darkness, and that we knew so well each winding of the place. Where the others are I do not know. Sir, help me! I am penniless, your police—blood-hounds!—are on my track. Every moment that I stay here makes the danger greater. To-day I am a creature you hate, scorn, shrink from; but yesterday I was the woman you loved—help me, then! I am young to die—I saved you! Answer, will you save me?"

"I will help you," said George Brudenell, quietly.

Time has effaced many things from Doctor Brudenell's memory, but it can never blot out his mental picture of that night—the drive through the silent street to the distant railway-station, from which a train could be taken to carry them to the sea, the waiting through the dragging hours until the tardy dawn broke, the fear, the stealth, the suspicion, the watching, the rapid flight through the early morning, that ended only when the blue water—so cruelly bright, untroubled, and tranquil it looked!—was audible and visible. Not a word had he spoken to his companion through the night, nor did either of them break silence until they stood upon the deck of the vessel which was to bear her to the New World which has rectified so many of the mistakes of the Old.

The deck was being cleared of those who were to return to the shore, when, for the last time, she turned her beautiful eyes upon his face.

"Farewell, Monsieur," she said, quietly; and he echoed:

"Farewell, Mademoiselle."

Good Mrs. Jessop never discovered which patient it was to whom her master had been called in the dead of the night, and who had kept him away for the best part of twenty-four hours; and she never could understand what that "foreign young woman"—a person concerning whom she was for a long time exceedingly voluble and bitter—could possibly mean by running off in that scandalous way. But there were several other things that Mrs. Jessop did not understand—for instance, why the doctor for the next few weeks lost his appetite so completely, was so "snappish and short," and seemed to care for nothing but the newspaper; and she was quite scandalized when he actually spent a whole day, as she, by dint of judiciously "pumping" Patrick, contrived to ascertain, in attending the trial of those "horrid wretches of dynamitards," where he heard the case, and heard the sentence of five years' penal servitude passed upon a gray-haired man with a scar upon his cheek.

Laura has come home now, and the children are a great deal bigger and even more tiresome than ever. She thinks her brother is very stupid not to marry, and often roundly tells him so. But the Doctor takes her suggestion very quietly; he is too old now, he says, and, besides, as he reminds Laura, it was never "in his line."